CREEP FROG

A SAMMY & BRIAN MYSTERY #7

BY KEN MUNRO

GASLIGHT PUBLISHERS

Creep Frog

Gaslight Publishers
P. O. Box 258
Bird-in-Hand, PA 17505

Library of Congress Number: 98-65122
International Standard Book Number: 1-883294-66-5

Printed 1998 by
Masthof Press
R. R. 1, Box 20, Mill Road
Morgantown, PA 19543-9701

DEDICATION

This book is for

All my fans
who tell me to
"keep them coming."

CHAPTER ONE

The man watched as the teenager emerged from an outside restroom. He glanced again at the damp and creased photograph he held in his clammy hand. Yes, this was definitely the one, the young boy he was to lure into The Old Wood Shop.

When Brian Helm left the coolness of the restroom behind the stores, the hot August sun and the tourists reminded him where he was. He and his best friend, Sammy Wilson, had been summoned to Kitchen Kettle Village to solve a mystery. The village was five miles east of Bird-in-Hand. It's thirty-two charming shops drew many tourists to the area. Now he had to find Sammy who was waiting for him somewhere in the crowd.

Brian emerged from between two shops and squirmed around some tourists. Then he stopped. A large man loomed over him, blocking his path. Brian stepped to the right. The man stepped to the right. Brian moved to the left. The man moved to the left. Brian frowned. Was someone playing a trick on him? His eyes shifted from the man's blue shirt up to his face. The stranger was not smiling.

The man, about forty, had a mustache and was bald except for patches of brown hair above each ear. He was six feet tall with muscular arms and shoulders. His opened-collar sport shirt revealed several heavy gold chains around his neck.

"Come with me," came a whisper as the man suddenly turned and created a path for Brian to follow. He passed several shops before he turned again and beckoned to the teenage boy.

On impulse, Brian hastened after the mysterious figure. The unexpected drama that was unfolding at the moment switched the young detective to his Secret Agent mode. His squinted eyes peered at the people roaming in and out of the nearby shops. Had they heard the whispered message? Did they suspect who he was? Did they know he was being recruited to serve on another dangerous mission?

When the tall man reached Newport Road next to the series of shops, he glanced back. The boy was still following him. He smiled for the first time. He couldn't believe his good luck. And yet he was disappointed. The teenager was supposed to be smart. Certainly not as brilliant and clever as his friend Sammy, but he was told Brian was not dumb.

Well, he would soon find out. They would all find out just how competent the super sleuths were.

Sammy Wilson studied the faces of the passing tourists. Next, he read the signs on the shops. Then he looked at his watch—again. Brian was late. This was not like Brian. He knew they had an appointment to meet Harry Clover, a maintenance man, about a problem at the Village.

As Sammy took his first step to retrieve Brian from the restroom, a teenage boy cornered him. "You're Sammy Wilson aren't you?" he asked, breathing heavily.

"Yes, I am. Why? What's wrong?"

The boy pointed his finger. "Some man grabbed Brian and dragged him into The Old Wood Shop down there."

"What do you mean, dragged?" asked Sammy, wanting more details to better analyze the situation.

"Brian was trying to get away, but the man had his hand over his mouth and pulled him into the shop. You better hurry."

Ignoring the boy's demand, the young detective glanced around for the nearest phone. He headed for the Gift Shop where Linda McFarland allowed the boy detective to use the store phone.

"Can you get word to him and tell him to meet me at The Old Wood Shop as soon as possible," said Sammy when told that Detective Ben Phillips was not at the police station. He handed the phone back to Linda, thanked her, and rushed outside.

If Brian's life was in danger, Sammy wanted to have Detective Phillips with him as insurance. But since Phillips was not available, Sammy would have to face this alone. He looked for the boy, but he was gone. The young detective headed for the wood shop.

The Old Wood Shop was on Newport Road, a block away from the shopping area of Kitchen Kettle Village. Like other businesses in the area, the wood shop started as a hobby in a home. Then as business grew, the house was enlarged and with internal changes was converted into a thriving enterprise.

The first thing that Sammy noticed was the "Closed" sign on the glass door. The teen shook his head. July was the peak of the tourist trade. No way should this place be closed, thought Sammy. Unless . . .

He cupped his hands around his face, leaned against the glass door, and looked in. The lights were off. No one was there. He tried the door. It was locked. He turned around, hoping that Detective Ben Phillips would be there. He was not.

Windows in the rear of the building looked into several work rooms. Sammy darted from one window to the next, hoping to see signs of Brian. But the rooms were empty except for piles of lumber, tools, and ready-to-assemble wood pieces. It was spooky. No people. No Brian. Just . . .

Movement.

Sammy shifted his position for a better look. A partially opened door led to a third room. Sammy could see the back of a man. The man moved to his left, unveiling someone tied to a chair. It was Brian!

Sammy's heart pounded. At least his friend was alive.

He ran to the front of the shop. Detective Phillips was nowhere in sight. Did he dare to break in and confront possible danger? He knew the police always waited for backup in situations like this. But what if Detective Phillips didn't get his message? Even if the detective got the message, maybe he would not be able to respond in time.

The super sleuth had to make a decision. He stopped some tourists across the street. He explained the situation and told them to call the police. He rushed back around to the windows, hoping one would be unlocked. The first window he tried opened. The area inside was next to the room with the opened door. He raised the window higher and quietly crawled inside.

Sammy maneuvered around a table saw and opened the door opposite the windows. It led to the store in front as he had suspected. He went and slowly opened the side door that led to the room with the opened door through which he had seen Brian. He glanced to his left at the doorway. From this angle Brian and the man were not visible. Good. That meant they couldn't see him as he slipped into the next room.

After carefully dodging stacks of unassembled pieces of wood, Sammy sneaked close to the opened door. He heard a voice.

"We'll hide you away then we'll get your friend, Sammy Wilson. How much money are you worth to your family?" The man laughed.

With his back against the wall, the teenage detective looked for something he could use as a weapon. A wheelbarrow handle would make a good club, thought Sammy. But what if the man had a gun?

Next he glanced at the plastic piping that ran across the ceiling from one workroom to the next. His eyes traced one four-inch pipe that led to a large container that collected sawdust from the various table saws and sanders. Sammy clinched his lips and nodded his head. He was developing a plan.

Returning to the first room, Sammy opened the door again that led into the store. He grabbed the door frame and stuck his head inside. He made a quick examination of the front door and the door to the right. That door led directly to the room where Brian was tied to the chair.

He pushed himself back and snatched up a screwdriver from a workbench. Using the screwdriver, he loosened the metal band that attached the flexible plastic pipe to the table saw. He then twisted and pulled the pipe until it popped off, sending sawdust into the air. He shook the pipe. More sawdust fell to the floor. Sammy waited a moment, took a deep breath, and then held the pipe to his face.

Two rooms away, a fifteen-year-old boy was trying to undo the rope that held him to the chair. Sweat ran down around his eyes and over the duct tape that covered his mouth. His arms were tired, his wrists rubbed red by the course fiber rope. Brian frowned. It always works in the movies, he thought. The hero tightens his muscles when he is tied up by the bad guy. Then later he relaxes his muscles and pulls his hands free from the slackened rope. If only I had muscles, thought Brian as he closed his eyes and hung his head.

"Don't expect your friend, Sammy, to help you," shouted the man. "He doesn't even know you're here."

Brian moaned and shook his head.

"Ha, ha," teased the man, producing a large grin.

The noise that came from the next room caused the smile to quickly vanish from the man's face.

"Help! Help me! I fell into the dust bin!" came a muffled voice.

The man spun around and rushed into the next room, looking for the location of the voice.

"Get me out of here," said the voice.

The man saw the large container with several plastic pipes leading from it. He rushed to the dust bin.

Brian tried to slide himself and the chair for a better view of the next room. But before he could make any headway, Sammy appeared through the other door. The tape covering Brian's mouth wrinkled into a smile.

The index finger at Sammy's mouth told Brian to be quiet. Sammy bent down to untie the rope, but Brian's escape attempt had tightened the knots. Sammy glanced at the door and wondered how long the man would be distracted. The sounds indicated the man was trying desperately to yank the pipes away from the sawdust receptacle.

Sammy twisted the strand of rope that came from the knot to make the rope thinner. He pushed on the rope to force it back through the knot. It worked! Five seconds later Brian was free.

"Come on. Let's get out of here," whispered Sammy.

Brian followed as his buddy headed back into the store. They rushed for the front door. But just as Sammy released the dead bolt, a large hand grabbed his shoulder.

"Where do you think you're going?" asked a deep ominous voice.

CHAPTER TWO

Sammy turned, hoping he wouldn't see a gun. His muscles were tense, his fists prepared to smash into flesh. Brian was quicker. He butted his head into the man's side. The man flinched and raised his hands as if to ward off any more blows to his body.

"Hey, hey. Stop! It's me. It's me."

The boys looked up at the six-foot-two, two-hundred-twenty-pound man. His thin mustache and receding hair line took second place to his penetrating eyes.

It was Detective Ben Phillips.

Brian waved his left arm and pointed. "There's a man in there, and he kidnapped me and he tied me up, and hurry so he doesn't get away," said Brian in one breath, stumbling over his words.

Before Phillips could respond, the man appeared in the doorway. "I'm not going anywhere," he coughed, sawdust flying everywhere. He smiled and raised a flaky, empty hand.

The room was still. The teenagers were trying to adjust to something that didn't make sense. They looked at Phillips.

The detective nodded. "Boys, meet Steve Springer, United States Marshal."

Brian shook his head. "You mean you really are a real federal marshal?"

The boys slowly stepped forward and reluctantly shook the extended hand.

"The marshal has a problem and needs your help," said Phillips.

Brian rubbed his sore wrists. "He has a problem all right. He snatches people from the street, ties them in chairs, and threatens them. He needs the the help of a shrink, not us."

"I'm sorry, but what I did was necessary," said Steve Springer. "I had to check out your reputation as amateur detectives. When Ben Phillips here told me about the cases you've solved and the tremendous help you've been to the police, I had to verify his claims."

"So you set up this kidnap scenario to test us," said Sammy.

"Exactly. I had to be certain that you were right for the job."

"What job?" asked Brian.

"Hey, wait a minute, boys," said Ben Phillips. "Let's find out first if you passed the test."

They all looked at Steve Springer for a clue. The marshal's face was not handing out clues at the moment.

"I guess we failed," said Brian. "I didn't believe you when you first showed me your shield and said you were a United States Marshal."

"That's why I had to grab you, drag you inside here, and tie you to the chair. The plan was to find out how you and Sammy would react to you being kidnapped."

Sammy brushed hair back from his eyes and glared. "So you sent that boy to tell me that Brian had been abducted by a stranger and taken into this building."

"Yes, and nobody was to get hurt," said Detective Phillips, sensing Sammy's irritation. "That's why I was here. I didn't want Mr. Springer's plan to get out of hand. If you think this was a bad idea, I'll take the blame. I was the one who told the marshal that you could handle it."

Sammy glanced at Brian who raised his eyebrows and shrugged. His first thoughts were that Brian and he had been used. The idea of having to pass a test did not appeal to him either. However, the thrill of the adventure was still vibrating throughout his body. He was pleased that they had impressed a United States Marshal. He relaxed. Now was the time for productive thinking and action, not self-pity. He looked at Phillips. "When I phoned you for help, you were already here," said Sammy.

"Yep. And you did the right thing. You called for backup help when you evaluated the situation."

"And, Sammy," said the marshal, patting the teen's shoulder, "using the pipe to carry your voice from one room to the next was ingenious. I honestly have to say, I really thought you had fallen into that sawdust box. I was scared because I knew Detective Phillips here would have my hide if anything had happened to you boys."

Ben Phillips smiled and shook Sammy's hand. "Well, I'd say you passed the test." He noticed the rejected look on Brian's face. "And, Brian . . ."

Brian pointed to Springer's hands. "Well, you'd think a real United States Marshal wouldn't have dirty fingernails, and the badge you showed me wasn't attached to a leather case, and . . ." He pointed to the marshal's neck. "And real feds wouldn't wear gold chains around their necks. A person could use them to choke you. How did you expect me to believe you were a real marshal?" Brian pouted.

"I didn't. And that's why you passed the test, too," replied Springer. "If you had believed me on face value, that would tell me you are naive and gullible. That's not the kind of people I want on my team."

Brian's face beamed. Team. I'm on his team, thought Brian. He stood tall, threw back his shoulders, and displayed the best posture he could muster.

But before Brian committed both of them to the "team," Sammy spoke up. "What's this job you're talking about?"

"Part of the responsibility of the United States Marshals Service is to protect witnesses who testify against organized crime. When their lives are threatened, we provide for the relocation and protection of the witness and his or her family. We take them from the dangerous area and move them to a new safe place, often in another state."

Brian, having shrunk back to his normal size and shape, said, "I don't see how you can hide someone by just moving him to another town in another state."

"There's more to it than that. We provide the person with a new name. We give him or her a new birth certificate, a new Social Security number, even redo his or her physical appearance."

"With plastic surgery," added Sammy.

"When necessary, right. And with a new hair style, colored contact lenses, and maybe a mustache or beard thrown in, that witness becomes a different person."

"How can Brian and I be of help to you?" asked Sammy.

"Well, we have a problem," said Springer, going to the window and scanning the people walking by. "Word is getting out where we are placing some of these people."

"There's a leak somewhere," said Sammy.

"And you want us to plug it up," added Brian.

"No, we'll do the plugging," said the marshal. "We have relocated a witness into this area of Lancaster County. I want you boys to find the family we placed here."

The room went quiet. Even Detective Ben Phillips was caught off guard.

"You have a family relocated here in the village?" asked the detective.

"That's right."

"You put them here and you lost them?" asked Brian.

"*We* know where they are. But can they be found by someone else? We have information that the man sent to prison knows that the witness works here in Kitchen Kettle Village. But, he doesn't know *where*." Springer slid his hand down over his face as if trying to make something go away. He sighed then said, "We have reason to believe that a thug is on his way here now to physically harm or even kill the witness. But, of course, he has to find him first."

Sammy gave that some thought then said, "You think the witness, because he has a new identity and a new face, cannot be found."

Springer nodded. "There are many houses in the Village and surrounding area. We believe we have our witness and his family so well hidden they cannot be found—even if word is out that they work here in Kitchen Kettle Village."

"However," said Sammy, "you want to be sure. So, you're going to challenge Brian and me to find the needle in the haystack. And if that needle can be found, you hope *we* find it before the thug does."

Springer nodded again. "We want to know how foolproof our system is. The lives of three people depend on it. Detective Phillips tells me, if it's possible for the witness to be found, you boys will do it. Well—do you accept the challenge?"

"Yes, sir," replied Brian, standing three inches taller and almost saluting. He glanced at his partner. "Right, Sammy?"

The challenge *was* everything Sammy could hope for. A real-life problem to solve—for the federal government. His mouth twitched as he was about to speak. He hesitated and examined Springer's face. More was going on here than the marshal indicted. Sammy felt it. "Never take anything at face value," said the little voice within.

All eyes were on Sammy.

Finally the teenage detective nodded.

The marshal smiled. He hurried to a nearby desk. From a drawer he withdrew some newspapers. "The name of the man you're looking for *was* Charles Parker. We're pressed for time. So here. This is all you get for a start." He passed the small bundle to Sammy. "These are the newspaper accounts of the trial. You could have found this information on your own by surfing the Internet. After you read these, you'll know almost as much as Mack Roni."

"Who's Mack Roni?" asked Brian.

"He's your adversary—the man being sent here to find the witness. He's known by the name Mack Roni."

"If you know who he is, why don't you arrest him?" asked Brian.

"That's the sad part. We can't do anything until he commits a crime."

"So you wait until he kills your witness then you arrest him," said Brian, smirking.

Springer rubbed his hand back over his bald head. "No, we catch him in the act of committing the crime, then we arrest him."

"Okay," said Sammy. "The witness's real name is Charles Parker, and these newspapers contain information about the trial. Is that it? Is this all we get to start?"

"That's it. And good luck."

"Are you wishing us good luck to find him or good luck not to find him?" asked Sammy.

Marshal Springer grinned. "What do you think?"

Sammy studied the expression on Springer's face. He couldn't be sure of the answer.

"Oh," said the marshal, reaching into his pocket, "here's my card with my phone number. Call me when you locate Charles Parker." Then with his hand on Detective Phillips' shoulder, he said, "Well, shall we go and leave these boys to their task at hand?"

When the U.S. Marshal came to Phillips a week ago, Phillips didn't hesitate to recommend Sammy and Brian for testing the security of the Witness Protection Program. Now that his young detective friends had the Marshals Service's stamp of approval, he was even more proud of the boys. However, he couldn't leave now without a comment.

"Sammy and Brian, you realize that if you can find the witness, that means there's a possibility that Mack Roni can also find him. Which means the witness and his family will have to be uprooted and located elsewhere. This is one time I hope you succeed by failing. But why is it I have a feeling Kitchen Kettle Village isn't going to be the same after this case is over?"

Sammy heard Phillips' comments, but his mind was working on unanswered questions. "Oh, one more thing," said Sammy. "This appointment Brian and I have with Harry Clover. Was that an excuse to get us here to the Village so we could be tested?"

"No, that was a stroke of luck," said Springer. "When I heard that Harry Clover was going to see you boys, I . . . well, used the opportunity." The marshal glanced at his watch. "You better get going. He might still be waiting for you."

"And what does Mr. Clover want to see us about?" asked Sammy, wanting to find out just how informed this man was.

"He wants to fool someone. I believe it has something to do with a frog."

"A frog?" said Brian.

"Yes, apparently someone kidnapped a frog."

CHAPTER THREE

S ammy and Brian reentered the area known as Kitchen Kettle Village. A favorite at the Village, Jimmy LaRue and his boys were strumming and singing. A crowd had gathered around the musicians. While some tourists didn't allow Banjo Jimmy to lure them from shopping, others either stood or settled into the bench seats provided nearby. The crowd swayed, hummed, or sang along to the old standards. The small peach basket displayed in front held the generous donations given by the pleased spectators.

They were late—really late. They were to have met Harry Clover over an hour ago in front of the Jam and Relish Kitchen. Would he still be waiting?

Sammy clasped the folder containing the news clippings tightly in his hand. He was eager to get home. This assignment that had unexpectedly been thrust upon them would take all of their time.

There was no way they could handle a new case. They would have to turn Harry Clover down.

As they neared the Jam and Relish Kitchen, it was no surprise that no one was waiting for them. The teen detectives wouldn't have recognized Harry Clover anyway, since the plea for help came by phone.

"Hey, Sammy. Hey, Brian," said a voice from behind.

The boys spun around.

The man was in his thirties and wore tan work clothes. His well-trimmed, brown hair gave emphasis to his blue-gray eyes. He hurried over to the boys. "Sorry I made you wait." I had to get my ten-cent cup of coffee." He pointed back to the sandwich shop. "It's the only place I know where you can still get coffee for ten cents."

If this man was Harry Clover, his tone of voice and leisurely manner gave no indication that he was mad at their being late.

"You're Harry Clover?" asked Sammy.

"Yeah." He motioned to an empty bench in front of the Jam and Relish Kitchen. "Let's sit over here. I want to explain something to you before we go up to the office." Between sips of coffee, Clover told his reason for phoning the amateur detectives. "I want you to help me. But keep it a secret. I want to play a joke on someone."

"A joke?" said Brian. "We don't . . ."

"Whom do you want to play this joke on?" asked Sammy.

"I . . . don't quite know," came the reply.

Sammy's eyebrows wrinkled. "You don't know the person you want to play the joke on?"

"Well, yes, I know the person I want to play the joke on, but I don't know who it is."

"What person are you talking about?" asked Sammy in desperation.

"I'm talking about the person who kidnapped the frog," came the answer.

Brian's blank face displayed an opened mouth.

So here it was, thought Sammy, the kidnapped frog. Sammy spoke slowly and deliberately. "Somebody kidnapped a frog, you don't know who it is, but you want to play a joke on that person."

"That's right. The frog was taken as a joke. But we don't know who did it. I want to turn the joke back on that person by bringing in two detectives to work the case. It will be a fun case, done for laughs. You'll be paid."

Sammy, deep in thought, waved his hand and said, "We don't charge for our detective work." Then as an afterthought, he said, "How do you know the frog was taken? Maybe it just hopped away."

"There was a ransom note," answered Harry.

"Do you have any idea who might have done it?" asked Brian.

"No," said Harry. "It could be anybody from the Village here. The frog was kept on a filing cabinet in the office. Most of the shopkeepers and employees here in the Village roam through the office at one time or another."

Sammy smiled. He had intended to refuse the case, but now he changed his mind. This would make a great cover for Brian and him to infiltrate the Village to find Charles Parker, the hidden witness.

As Jimmy LaRue was singing something about Bill Bailey coming home, Brian was trying to visualize a frog on a filing cabinet. "Was the frog kept in a wire cage?" he asked.

"Before this develops into an Abbott and Costello routine," announced Harry, "this is a green, plaster of Paris frog we're talking about. It's not a real frog. It's about fifteen inches long and a foot high."

"Why would someone steal a frog made of plaster?" asked Brian.

"That's my point," said Harry. "It must have been a joke. What else?"

Sammy produced a notebook and pen from his pocket. He placed the notebook on top of the folder that rested on his lap. "Suppose you start at the beginning and tell us about this frog."

Harry pointed to his left. "When I first started working here, there used to be a small pond over there. Tourists would throw coins into it and make a wish. When enough coins accumulated, the money was donated to a worthy cause. Well, in the center of the pond was a green, plaster of Paris frog. The frog was different, kind of homely looking and creepy. Tourists would look twice at the frog, making sure that what they saw was what they saw. When the pond was relocated to another part of the Village, the frog was retired to the office."

"What do you mean, retired?" asked Brian.

"The receptionist, Lynne Trout, kind of adopted the ugly thing. She cleaned it and dressed it up as a conversation piece. One day she'll have a fresh flower taped to its head. Several days later the frog is wearing a small homemade bikini swimsuit. The people who come into the office smile and get a kick out of it. Some days the frog wears sunglasses; other days it holds a small American flag."

The smile vanished from Harry's face. "Three days ago the frog disappeared. In its place was a typed ransom note. It said not to call the police or we'd never see the frog again."

"Yeah, somebody's playing a joke all right," said Brian.

Harry stood. "Come on, I'll take you upstairs to the office. I want you to meet a couple of people."

Trees throughout the Kitchen Kettle Village provided much appreciated shade on hot August days. Every time Jimmy LaRue stopped traffic with his foot-stomping music, the shaded seats filled quickly. The low stone wall under the large oak tree, which also shaded the musicians, provided adequate seating. However, the prime location was the curved wooden bench that circled another oak tree, twenty feet away, but directly in front of the musicians.

The fifty-year-old man, his wife, and nineteen-year-old son were lucky. They had seats on the curved bench. But only the wife was enjoying herself. The son was squirming about, moving his head left and right. The father's deep-set eyes were also searching but in a slow, deliberate manner. He finally focused on two teenage boys and a man about to enter the Jam and Jelly Kitchen. The man smiled as he smoothed back his bushy eyebrows with his thumb and middle finger. He leaned back and allowed his right foot to join the rhythm of Jimmy's song. Now he could relax. He had identified the boys who would establish the trail to Charles Parker.

CHAPTER FOUR

Harry marched the boys through the store and headed for the steps that led to the office above. Brian gawked at the displays. Countless jars of jellies, jams, and relishes were everywhere. Each display had its own opened jars and crackers for tasting. Woven baskets hung from the ceiling. Two check-out counters handled the busy crowd.

Brian watched as tourists put jam on fresh crackers and sampled the different flavors. His mouth watered. Boy was he hungry. He saw a vacant tasting spot and moved in.

He grabbed a cracker and a spoon and went for it. He flopped the fruity mass onto the little cracker. The glob of jelly overran the cracker and oozed down his fingers. Brian quickly dropped the spoon, side stepped, and brought his free hand up to catch the dripping mess. At that moment his elbow jabbed a tourist, who backed up into a woman, who was about to sample her jelly-topped cracker. The lady was later heard to comment that it was hard to breathe with jelly up your nose.

Sammy looked back at the commotion. He lowered his shaking head. He brought a hand up and covered his eyes. Did he dare admit that this troublemaker was his friend. "Come on, Brian," he finally whispered through the tourists.

The stern look on Sammy's face told Brian he'd better head for the steps, fast. "Hmm, strawberry," he said to himself as he swallowed the last of the cracker and then licked his fingers.

The overhead sign said, "Welcome to our kit-chen! Today we are cooking—Strawberry Preserves."

In the back half of the store to the right was a bakery. To the left was the opened kitchen where stainless steel kettles cooked the fruits. Steam rose from the many pots. Tourists watched as Amish girls operated the funnel filler. The funnel filled individual jars with jam. These filled jars were then placed into a hot water bath that killed any bacteria and created a vacuum seal.

Brian hurriedly took a peek as he scampered up the steps after his buddy.

"Sammy and Brian, this is Pat Burnley," said Harry.

The woman, tall and in her seventies, stood at her office door. She smiled and extended her hand. "I've heard those names before," she said as she shook the boys' hands. She raised a sticky hand to her nose. "Ah, strawberry." She looked at Brian. "You have good taste."

"Mrs. Burnley created Kitchen Kettle Village," said Harry. "She started her business by making small batches of jelly on gas burners in a garage forty-four years ago."

"Gee, the jelly doesn't taste that old," said Brian without smiling.

Only Sammy knew that Brian meant it as a joke. Harry wasn't sure. He quickly said, "This is Sammy Wilson and Brian Helm, Bird-in-Hand's amateur detectives," said Harry. "I've hired them to find the frog."

The surprised look on Pat Burnley's face was not lost on Sammy.

But just as quickly Pat developed a broad smile and shook her head. "When we built the pond, I had two frogs exactly alike. I filled the one with candy and gave it to a granddaughter who collects frogs. The other one was placed in the pond. My granddaughter's frog broke so only one frog is left."

"Don't worry," said Brian, developing his secret agent posture. "We'll find it for you."

Mrs. Burnley smiled graciously as though Brian's words just solved all her problems. She glanced up toward the next room. "Lynne, come over here."

Lynne Trout appeared from her office. A woman in her early fifties, she was short, hefty, and had a broad smile on her face.

"Lynne is our receptionist," said Mrs. Burnley. "She is super at handling complaints. She also takes a personal interest in all our employees—*and frogs.* She's the one you want to talk to."

Lynne looked surprised. But she didn't allow Pat Burnley's words to divert her curiosity.

"What do you think of this, Lynne?" Pat continued, "Harry has hired two detectives to find the missing frog."

Lynne looked at the "boy" detectives and grinned in recognition. "Sammy and Brian! I read about you two in the newspapers. Welcome to Kitchen Kettle Village." She shot Harry a glance. Then with a straight face she said, "The note said we weren't to call in the police."

Sammy noticed the twinkle in Lynne's eyes. She was playing along with the joke. And quite well, too.

Harry smiled. "That's just it. They aren't the police. They're amateur detectives."

Lynne laughed. "I think Harry wants to test your reputation as crime solvers." The smile vanished as she turned and in a mysterious tone, said, "Follow me. I'll show you the crime scene— and the ransom note."

Pat Burnley stayed behind as the teenagers and Harry trailed after the receptionist.

The room was small but had a desk with a computer, a bookcase, supply closet, and a filing cabinet.

Lynne pointed to the metal cabinet. Then filled with all the sadness and grief she could muster, she sighed and said, "And this is where froggie was when she was kidnapped."

Sammy was impressed. Lynne Trout was quite an actress. The only thing missing were the tears.

"And the ransom note?" asked Brian.

"Right here," she said, producing a paper from her desk.

She handed the note to Sammy, who read the message aloud. "Your frog has been kidnapped. Do not call the police or you will never see the frog again."

Brian removed a blank sheet of paper from the desk. He held the paper next to the note.

"Hmm," said Sammy. "Same paper."

"And I bet the note was typed on this," said Brian as he tapped the top of the computer with his free hand. He glanced at Lynne to get her reaction.

"No, I'm afraid not," said Sammy. "Look here. These letters are indented into the paper. This note was written on a typewriter."

Brian scanned the room for a typewriter. He frowned when he saw none.

When Sammy noticed that Lynne wasn't going to make it easy for them, he asked, "Are there any typewriters around here?"

She nodded. "There's one in the work room."

Then with a sly smile she added, "Of course, it's available for anyone to use."

"I see," said Sammy. "Harry told us earlier that the shopkeepers and maintenance people are in and out of here all the time."

"Yep," nodded Lynne.

Great! This is what Sammy was hoping for. Now he and Brian would have an excuse to interview everyone in the village. While they searched for the kidnapped frog, they might just turn up the relocated witness. Sammy smiled. He added the ransom note to the news clippings already in the folder. "You don't mind if I take the ransom note, do you?"

Lynne shook her head.

"Does this mean you're taking the case?" asked Harry.

"Absolutely," replied Sammy.

CHAPTER FIVE

Sammy's bedroom was home base for the aspiring teenage detectives. Most of their productive thinking and planning was done there. It was officially known as the Brainstorming Room. The room next to the bedroom contained shelves of books and lab equipment. That was the Research Room.

Half an hour after he divided the news clippings between Brian and himself, Sammy leaned back and examined his notes. Brian, belly down on the floor next to the bed, was still reading his share of the year-old articles from Arizona.

The *Phoenix Sun* headlines told the story. PROMINENT BANKER ARRESTED. VINCENT BRUNO ACCUSED OF LAUNDERING DRUG MONEY. BANKER TO GO ON TRIAL. ACCOUNTANT TO GIVE TESTIMONY. CHARLES PARKER TELLS OF DRUG MONEY DISTRIBUTION. VINCENT BRUNO IS CONVICTED—GETS 10 YEARS.

ACCOUNTANT RECEIVES THREATS. U.S. MARSHALS PUT CHARLES PARKER IN WITNESS PROTECTION PROGRAM.

Brian's snickering took Sammy's attention away from his notes. "What's so funny?" asked Sammy, shifting his chair to the side to get a better view of Brian.

"I was reading where Vincent Bruno says he's innocent. He accuses his accountant, Charles Parker, of stealing money from the bank. He says that Parker knew that Vincent was about to have him arrested for embezzlement. And that's why Parker made up the story that Vincent Bruno was laundering drug money."

Sammy smiled, "Yeah, I read that, too. But the evidence said otherwise. And besides, if it was true that Charles Parker did embezzle money from the bank, he wouldn't be in the Witness Protection Program. He'd be in jail along with Bruno."

Brian pointed to a photograph showing Charles Parker entering the courthouse. "I guess it won't do any good to study these pictures of Charles Parker. The way Mr. Springer talked, we wouldn't recognize him with his new face."

Sammy folded his arms across his chest and took a deep breath. A hint of a smile crossed his lips. "But there are some things they can't change about him."

Brian rolled over on his side and propped his head up with his elbow. "What's that?" he asked.

"They can't change his personality, his past experiences, or his habits," said Sammy, guiding his chair back behind his desk.

Brian glanced down at the newspapers. "I don't see any of those things in these pictures or mentioned in the articles," answered Brian.

"But we know he has experience as an accountant," added Sammy.

"Hey, that's right," said Brian, sitting up, placing his back against the bed. Slowly his face lost its glow. "You don't think we'll find him doing accounting at Kitchen Kettle Village do you?"

"Probably not, but he might be some kind of financial adviser. He could even be a math teacher."

Brian jumped to his feet. "Hey, right. Let's check the schools to see if they hired any new math teachers recently," he said.

"And then what?" asked Sammy.

"Well, then, he's the . . ."

The grin on his friend's face caused Brian to nod. "Yeah, yeah, I know. We don't accuse anyone without proof."

"Which brings us to the core of our problem," said Sammy. "If we do find our transplanted witness, how are we going to prove he's Charles Parker? Remember, he has a new identity and papers to prove it."

Brian stepped over the news articles and went behind the desk. He patted his friend's shoulder. "But you'll find a way. Right, Sammy?"

The smile on Brian's face was in contrast to Sammy's feelings. He felt the burden of everyone always expecting him to come up with the right answers. He accepted the responsibility, but with it came tension. The challenge and the resulting suspense gave him the motivation and energy that drove him forward. And that's what made him function at his best. Sammy excelled under pressure.

Scanning his notes, he stopped half way down the page. There it was. He rested his finger on the pad and glanced up at Brian. "Maybe this is our answer."

Brian smiled as he read the information. "Yeah, he has a wife named Lois and a son, Adam, who's eight years old. Correction, he's probably nine by now. So when we find our man, we . . ." He stopped and shuffled through Sammy's half of the newspapers. He left the desk and flopped down at the clippings on the floor. He searched all the photographs that accompanied the newspaper accounts of the trial. "But we don't know what his wife and son look like. They aren't in any of these pictures."

"Hmm," said Sammy. He swiveled his chair to face the computer and turned it on. When it booted up, the mouse clicked its way to the Internet.

Brian, who by this time was standing at Sammy's side, knew better than to ask any questions. He watched and waited as his buddy logged onto the *Phoenix Sun's* home page.

"Most newspapers have posted editions that go back ten years," said Sammy. "Let's see if Charles Parker's name comes up for any articles other than the trial."

The young detectives stared at the computer screen while Sammy's fingers searched out certain keys on the keyboard.

Brian waited as his friend's flying fingers finally came to a stop. "Boy, with all of that action, we should be in the White House now, watching the President conduct top secret negotiations."

"Very funny," said Sammy, his mind concentrating on the business at hand. He scrolled the information and studied the information. He reviewed the dates on the newspapers on his desk. His eyes returned to the screen. "Nothing new here. His name comes up for only the articles related to the trial."

"What were you expecting to find under his name?" asked Brian.

"His son was eight years old. He could have gotten married a year or two before his son was born. I thought maybe we might come up with a wedding picture."

Brian nodded. "How about his wife? Check under Lois Parker."

"Yeah, that's next," said Sammy as his fingers again mastered the keyboard.

The monitor reacted to the teenager's instructions.

"Well, well, well, look at this," said Sammy.

Displayed on the screen was a picture of a woman sitting in a chair and surrounded by flowers. The caption beneath the photo stated: Lois Parker relaxes among the many flower arrangements she creates in her home.

Sammy downloaded the news item onto the hard disc. He clicked on the word print and waited as the printer whirled into action. Two sheets of paper slid out containing the five-year-old article.

Neither of the boys said anything as Sammy laid the printout on the desk and they read the news article.

> Flowers galore fill a special room in Lois Parker's house. Since her husband built the greenhouse room two years ago, Lois has grown many varieties of flowers. What started as a hobby of making floral arrangements and giving them away to friends has now become an in-home business. "I make arrangements for hospitals, churches, and weddings now. It's almost too much. I'm going to have to cut back," said Mrs. Parker. It all started when Lois put a potted plant at the window. Then she added more pots, more flowers. Today, she raises fourteen varieties of flowers. And until she decides otherwise, the sweet smell of success will linger in the Parker household.

Sammy was first to finish reading. "Because of this article, it might be easier to track down Mrs. Parker rather than Mr. Parker," he said.

"Yeah, we look at the flower shop in the Village," replied Brian. "I bet it's her. And maybe her husband is helping run the business."

"It's worth a shot," said Sammy. "Of course her hair style will probably be different. Might even be another color." Sammy studied the picture that accompanied the article. "And her face will look five years older."

"Maybe even older," said Brian. "Going through a trial, having your life threatened, and being forced to move can make you age quickly."

"And another thing," added Sammy. "If Charles Parker himself built the flower room for his wife, he could be a carpenter or a woodworker."

"Right," said Brian. "Hey, let's go. What are we waiting for? Remember we have to get to the witness before the thug finds him."

"It's too late now," said Sammy, looking at his watch. "The shops close in half an hour."

Brian was disappointed, but as an afterthought, said, "Do you think Mr. Roni found this article about Lois Parker?"

"We have to assume he did," said Sammy. "Plus, I'm wondering what else Mr. Mack Roni knows that we don't know."

CHAPTER SIX

T he morning was bright and warm—a typical August day. Many cars and buses had already arrived and unloaded. By ten o'clock the area was alive with tourists, who allowed themselves to be wooed by the thirty-some specialty shops that were Kitchen Kettle Village.

Surrounding this shopper's paradise were many houses plus plenty of Amish farmland. A million tourists, wanting to witness the simple life, came to Lancaster County each year to see the Amish plow their fields with real horse power. They were amused at the Amish, riding their scooters by the side of the road. They were also enchanted by the rhythm of the horse and buggies. They marveled as the Amish passengers tried not to be intimidated by the faster vehicles that passed them by.

One visitor was not here to experience the Amish. Nor was he on vacation. He was working.

The stranger looked very ordinary—for a hoodlum. He was not a large man, but living a life outside the law made him tough and ruthless, a man to be feared. His appearance and manners sent a message that he was not to be messed with.

He was on a mission. The magnetic attraction of the Amish and the stores would not distract him from his assignment. It was payback time. He must find Charles Parker and settle the score for sending Vincent Bruno to jail.

As he approached the shops, he whistled a happy tune and glanced again at the papers in his hand. The first sheet contained pictures of Charles Parker as he was and computer-morphed photos with changes to his face and hair. The second paper noted possible occupations that Parker might have considered for his new, relocated lifestyle.

The man started with the first occupation listed: piano, music, musician. A nearby bulletin board displayed the names and locations of the village shops. He scanned the list, looking for a music shop. There it was, The Grande-Place, Music Boxes.

The Grande-Place was on the second floor, above Crimson & Clover, which sold bath soaps and body creams. A player piano was electronically flooding the store with nostalgia. The music brought memories and smiles to the tourists.

The stranger's face was hard, cold, unemotional. His mind was not on frivolous tunes, although when he was nervous, he was known to whistle a particular melody over and over. At the moment he was searching for an employee hired within the last year. A man who could play the piano.

"Hello, may I help You?" asked Al Lowrey, who along with his wife and sons ran the business.

A hint of a smile cracked its way across the stranger's face. "I'm looking for an old buddy of mine. I was told he got a job this past year in one of the shops here in the Village."

"What's his name?" asked Al.

"Ah, er, um, I don't know his real name. I always called him . . . Steinway. You know, because he played the piano."

"I have a man who's been working for us," said Al. "He fixes pianos at his home."

"Where's he live?" asked the man, sounding mysterious and anxious.

Al cast a suspicious glance at the stranger whose eyes were leaking revenge. "I'm sorry, but I don't give out personal information about my employees."

Linda Lowrey, Al's wife, was trying to get her husband's attention. She raised her hand and her voice. "Al, over here!"

Al welcomed the interruption. "I'm sorry. My wife wants me to help her move a display. So, if you'll excuse me."

The man wanted to stick his fist down Al's throat and say, "No, I won't excuse you." But he knew better. He couldn't make a scene. He had to keep a low profile if he wanted to continue the search for Charles Parker.

He noticed a door at the rear of the shop marked OFFICE. That's where the records would be, he thought. Records, which would have the names and addresses of all the employees. He wandered over to one of the front windows, pretending to examine the music boxes. Outside the window was a balcony and limbs of an oak tree which stretched high above the building. One limb came close to the window. He turned and took one last look at the shop's layout. He smiled, and then whistling a simple tune, walked down the stairs and vanished into the crowd of tourists.

At the same time, two bicycles were being chained to a post in the parking lot. The five-mile trip from Bird-in-Hand to Kitchen Kettle Village had taken Sammy and Brian about twenty minutes. They had ridden carefully because the tourist traffic traveling the Old Philadelphia Pike was heavy at times. But the sight of the rolling hills of Amish farmland and fresh air had made it a pleasant jaunt.

"Remember, Brian," said Sammy, "our strategy is to interview these people about the frog kidnapping, while keeping our eyes open for Charles Parker."

Brian thought back to yesterday. "Lynne Trout didn't seem to be upset about Harry hiring us to find the frog. So I guess she didn't take it."

"Maybe not," said Sammy, "but somebody's going to be upset when we start nosing around the Village."

The aroma from the flowers reached the aspiring detectives before the shop came into view. Sammy tried to identify the flowers by their fragrance.

Brian had other thoughts. He quickly became Helm, Brian Helm, alias, double-oh-seven and a half. He had visions of recognizing the shop owner as Lois Parker. He would confront her about the Witness Relocation Program. Then, at the mercy of his special interrogation techniques, she would confess, telling him where her husband could be found. Yes, and with his friend Sammy following behind, he would report to Marshal Steve Springer, that through clever detective work, he had located the witness.

Brian's bubble burst when the two boys got closer to the shop. If the old lady outside watering the potted flowers was the owner, no way was she Lois Parker.

"Hi," said Sammy as he nodded his head and smiled. "Are you the owner of the flower shop?"

The petite lady, in her sixties, stopped watering the geraniums and turned, facing the young boys. "Yes, I am," she answered. "I'm Mary Jane Mowrer."

"We're Sammy Wilson and Brian Helm," said Sammy. "We're investigating the missing frog."

"Oh, that's just a joke," laughed Mrs. Mowrer. "Somebody took it for fun. It'll turn up one of these days."

"Yes, I guess it will," said Sammy. "By the way, do you have anyone helping you here at the shop?"

"Why, yes, Amy. She does a lot of my flower arrangements. She'll be here tomorrow if you want to talk to her."

"How old is she? How long has she worked for you?" asked Brian, wanting to get to the bottom line.

Mrs. Mowrer looked up and to her right. "Amy's in her thirties. I'd say she's been here a year. You don't think she took the frog, do you?"

Sammy shook his head. Then as an afterthought asked, "Does she ever talk about Arizona?"

"No, not that I recall."

"Well, thank you for your help," said Sammy, leaving Mary Jane wondering what Arizona had to do with the missing frog.

Brian grinned as they walked away. "Do you think Amy is Lois Parker?"

"Maybe. We'll come back tomorrow," answered Sammy.

Then suddenly, changing the subject as Brian was known to do, he said, "Hey, let's have our picture drawn."

In front of the next shop, an artist, advertising quick portraits, was making a charcoal sketch of a young girl. A small group of people had gathered. They watched as the artist, an older lady, applied strokes, curves, and smudges of charcoal and chalk to the grayish paper. Smiles and nods appeared as the resemblance to the model became apparent.

Before Sammy could answer Brian's impulsive request, he heard a commotion. A crowd was gathering around a demonstration booth. "Come on, Brian, let's see what's happening."

The amateur sleuths arrived just in time. The man holding the knife had the attention of the spectators. He was in his late forties, tall and hefty. His brown hair was combed straight back.

Before he used the knife, he looked out over the crowd. "Well, well," he said, "look who's here today. You people are in for a treat." He pointed with his empty hand. "It's Sammy and Brian, the famous amateur detectives from Bird-in-Hand."

Sammy recognized the individual and was embarrassed by the introduction. Brian beamed radiantly. He liked being a celebrity. But before Brian did something foolish, Sammy squeezed his arm and whispered, "Brian, if you take a bow or say anything, I'll disown you."

Brian, who was ready to wave to the folks, thought better of it.

The tourists' attention now drew back to the man with the knife. He did not disappoint the crowd. He plunged his knife down and pierced the soft, warm outer skin. He twisted the long strip he had sliced and inserted it back. He hurriedly made five more cuts, twisted them and replaced them back into the cut area. The knife slit, sliced, and slithered. The man swirled, curled, and twisted. The people gasped with astonishment. John, the candle man, was well on his way to creating a decorative candle adorned with striking twists and curls, exposing colorful layers of wax.

When the attractive candle was finished, John sold it to the lady who had requested it. Customers lined up to purchase other candles.

The candle demonstration booth displayed ready-made candles of various shapes and sizes. Rings of artificial flowers were also available to further decorate each candle. Louise, John's partner, handled the remaining sales while he relaxed.

Sammy and Brian gazed at John and Louise. The super sleuths had met the two while working their last case, *Fright Train*. But that was last month. Could they be Charles and Lois Parker? How long have they had the candle booth? The woman looked younger than Lois. And John, the candle man, was heavier than Charles, the accountant. The extra weight could be part of Parker's physical reconstruction program. This was not going to be easy, thought Sammy as Brian and he approached the booth.

John extended his hands. "Okay, boys, you got me. I give up. Slap the handcuffs on and drag me to the slammer." A smile crossed his face. "I confess. I kidnapped the frog." He then produced a deep, hearty laugh.

Sammy was aware of John's humor but was surprised that word had spread so quickly. Evidently every employee of Kitchen Kettle Village knew that Bird-in-Hand's boy detectives were on the kidnapped-frog case. Well, good, he thought. While they're thinking frog, we'll be thinking Charles Parker.

Brian, not to miss an opportunity at humor himself, stood tall to display his secret agent image. "John, your big mistake came when you left pieces of candle wax on the filing cabinet." Brian's melodramatic voice deepened. "And a hidden camera captured your every move. We have a beautiful 8 by 10 blowup of you snatching the frog."

"Really? Great!" said John, returning the humor. "I'll take three copies."

Sammy was in no mood for humor right now. They had little time to find Charles Parker before Mack Roni found him. Wanting to catch the candle man off guard, Sammy quickly asked, "Is Williams Air Force Base still operating in Arizona?"

John's face went blank as if searching for the answer. Or, maybe John wouldn't allow the teenager to trick him. "I have no idea. Why do you ask?"

"Aren't you originally from Arizona?" asked Sammy, watching for any hint of deception.

"No, no, I always lived in Pennsylvania," replied the candle maker.

"Oh, okay," said Sammy, "my mistake."

John gestured with one hand and picked up a candle core with the other. "See you detectives later. I have to get back to work."

As the boys repositioned themselves for a better view, the candle man started his spiel. "We take this six-point candle core and redip it thirty times into these vats containing ten different colored wax. We go from the hot wax to the cold water with every dip which . . ."

A new batch of tourists quickly gathered. They watched and listened as John, the candle man, skillfully guided his knife through the multi-colored layers of warm wax.

But the man with bushy eyebrows and deep-set eyes wasn't watching the candle maker. His eyes were on Sammy and Brian. He moved in next to Sammy, bringing his wife and son with him. At the same time young boy stationed himself on the other side of Brian.

Even though Sammy was concentrating on John's artistry, he became aware of the sudden intrusion. He wondered why this man insisted on standing so close. After all, this was not a Garth Brooks concert. When Sammy displayed his polite get-out-of-my-space glance, it was apparent that the tourist was more interested in Brian and him than in the candle man.

"Hello," said the man, smiling. "I heard the guy say that you two are Sammy and Brian, amateur detectives from Bird-in-Hand."

Brian tilted his head to get a better view of the stranger. Probably a fan, wanting an autograph, thought the teenager. He felt for the special "autograph" pen he always carried in his pocket but never used.

"Yes, we are. We sometimes work with the police," answered Sammy.

"We're staying at the Bird-in-Hand Family Inn. I'm in the security business myself. The name's Glen Rock," replied the man, his bushy eyebrows rising, producing a rippled forehead. He stepped back. "This is my wife, Shirley, and my son, Glen Junior. We're on vacation."

The teenage detectives smiled and nodded. Brian was ready to whip out his autographing pen, but when nothing else was said, he broke the silence. "Where are you from?"

"Ohio. Not too far away," said Glen Rock.

Sammy's concentration was now refocused. Instead of the candle man, he was more interested in this man who deliberately placed himself next to them and insisted on being friendly. This man *is* after something, thought Sammy. Did Glen Rock want to hire them for his security business? While Sammy waited for that scenario to present itself, he glanced at the wife, Shirley.

Shirley Rock seemed distant from her husband. Her attention was on the man turning

an ordinary candle into a colorful creation. She
went through the motions and responded to her
husband's chatter, but found the candle maker's
world more appealing.

Next, Sammy looked at Glen Junior. He was
searching the crowd for something or someone.
But what? Who?

The nineteen-year-old caught Sammy
inspecting him. Without shifting gears, the boy
asked, "Do you have any gambling going on in
this area?"

Brian responded. "Yeah, try driving on Rt.
30 East."

Glen Junior, not understanding the local
joke, asked innocently, "Oh, you have casinos?"

"No," said Sammy, "Brian was joking."

The fast-growing, fascinated crowd listened
as John continued, ". . . and we have eight different
candle designs we sculpture. You may choose the
color and design at no extra charge . . ."

"Is this your first time here?" asked Brian.

A nudge from his friend's elbow told Brian
he should stay quiet.

"Yes, it is. Actually it was my son's idea to
come up here. He talked his mother into
suggesting that we take a trip to see the Amish.
And, I had business up this way so here we are."

"Burning instructions come with each
purchase," John was announcing to the potential
customers. "One of the keys, to keep the flame
from destroying the outside of the candle, is to

trim the wick down one quarter inch after burning the candle. Now, this large candle . . ."

Glen Rock bumped Sammy's arm to keep his attention. "Are you working on a case now? Is that why you're here?" he asked.

Brian was ready to answer, but he could still feel the effects of Sammy's elbow.

Sammy was not surprised when the man asked such a personal question. "No, we're just visiting," he said. Taking hold of Brian's arm he walked away and added, "I hope you and your family enjoy your visit here."

Glen Rock looked surprised but made no attempt to stop them. He simply replied, "We're going to take the horse and wagon tour next. Is it worth the time?"

"Yes, you can learn a lot about this area and the Amish," said Sammy without breaking his stride. He and Brian weaved back through the spectators. Soon the young detectives were free from the smothering effects of the large gathering and of Glen Rock.

However, they were not yet free from John's fading voice. "The last phase of candle making is to dip the finished candle into this clear hot wax which acts as a sealant. I dip the candle. Now everything is set and ready to go . . ."

Brian saw the concern on his buddy's face. "They're just tourists from Ohio. Right, Sammy?"

With the candle man's last words still ringing in his ear, Sammy had doubts. "Brian, keep your eyes on them. See where they go, what they do."

"But we have to find Mr. Parker," said Brian. "Aren't we going to investigate more shops here in the Village?"

"I'll do that while you watch Glen Rock." The returning frown told Sammy that his friend didn't like that idea. "Hey, they might lead you to Mr. Parker," he added.

"Aren't you Sammy and Brian?" asked a shy voice.

It was the boy who had been standing alongside of Brian.

"Yeah, we are," said Brian as he automatically whipped out his autograph pen. "I guess you want our autograph."

Sammy closed his eyes and shook his head.

"Ah, yeah, that's neat," said the boy, searching his pockets for a scrap of paper. He finally produced a paper containing names and addresses. The name Rainbow Dinner Theater was on top. "Here," said the boy, turning the paper over.

Brian signed his name first. Sammy glanced at the paper's front side before he signed his name on the back under Brian's name. "Do you like to see the plays at the Rainbow Dinner Theater?" Sammy asked as he returned the autographed paper.

"Yeah, and I get all the actors' autographs. Your names will be my first detective autographs."

He returned the paper to his pocket. "Ah, I want to go home, but I'm not sure which way to go. I just moved here several months ago. I wasn't supposed to leave the house today, but I came here to see my father. He works here. Can you help me get home?"

"How old are you?"asked Sammy.

"Nine," replied the boy.

"You're nine years old, you moved here several months ago, and your father works here in the Kitchen Kettle Village," repeated Sammy.

Brian looked at Sammy.

Sammy looked at Brian.

CHAPTER SEVEN

hat's your name?" asked Sammy, not really expecting the boy to say Adam Parker.

"Ah, Justin Groff."

"Where do you live?" asked Brian, already visualizing facing Marshal Steve Springer and handing him the new name and correct address of Charles Parker and his family.

"Two hundred seven Main Street," said Justin. "It's a white house."

"Well, let's find your house right now," said Brian, sounding like a big brother.

"Brian, don't you have a job to do?" asked Sammy. "I'll take care of Justin. I'll meet you back at the Jam and Relish House."

"But, you . . . But I . . . But we don't have to . . ."

As the blue in Sammy's eyes grew dark and threatening, Brian wrapped himself in his security blanket. He became Secret Agent Helm. And to let Sammy know he did not appreciate the situation, he saluted and said, "All right, sir. I understand, sir. You go right ahead, sir, while I keep my eye on . . ."

Something was wrong. Glen Rock, his wife, and son were gone. Brian quickly dropped his secret agent act and frantically scanned the crowd. The Rocks weren't there. He looked back for Sammy and the boy. They were gone, too. Now he was alone—except for hundreds of tourists.

Justin smiled as the white house, his house, came into view.

The clapboard structure was old like others in the area. While it was neat and well maintained, the house was plain. The windows had scant curtains with drawn blinds. Flowers were absent from the yard. The grass was balding from old age. The house had settled into retirement. It looked cold and lonely even on this hot August day with plenty of tourists milling about.

"That's my house. Thanks for your help." And with that, Justin Groff ran in and closed the door.

Sammy hadn't expected Justin to bolt away so quickly. He wanted to ask the boy about his father, about his mother. But now the opportunity was gone.

It was all very mysterious. Was this the home of Charles Parker and his family? Sammy wondered. Was the mother at home, or was the boy alone? Did boredom cause Justin Groff to seek temporary freedom at Kitchen Kettle Village? And did he seek out his father to ease the loneliness he must feel?

No matter, Sammy had the name—Groff. He would simply inquire whether the Village employed anyone by that name.

When Sammy arrived at the Jam and Relish House, Brian was not there. He assumed Brian was hot on Glen Rock's trail. The super sleuth decided to visit Lynne Trout upstairs in the business office.

"Nobody works here by the name of Groff, man or woman," said the receptionist, much to Sammy's sorrow.

Lynne gave Sammy a sly look. "Is that who kidnapped the frog?"

"I'm not sure yet," said Sammy. "You know this area pretty well. What can you tell me about the house at 207 Main Street? It's a white clapboard building. The one between the two brick houses."

"I believe the Johnsons live there," answered Lynne. "Fred and Agnes Johnson."

Sammy didn't want to hear that. "Do they have a nine-year-old boy?" he asked.

Lynne laughed. "No, their children are out on their own. Fred and Agnes must be in their seventies."

"Justin Groff could be their grandson," suggested Sammy. "Maybe they have a daughter and her family is living with them. And the daughter's married name is Groff," said Sammy, pleased with himself.

"Yes, that's possible," said Lynne, "but what does that have to do with our stolen frog? Do they have it?"

Sammy's blank expression told Lynne not to expect a reply.

Lynne Trout stood with her arms folded in front. "Hey, I'm not hard to get along with. Tell them if they return the frog, we will pay a reward. No questions asked." The stern tone of her voice indicated she was imitating an insurance investigator from a bad movie.

Sammy smiled at Lynne's unique personality and started down the steps. "I'll be sure to deliver that message to the guilty party."

Outside, Sammy found Brian waiting for him. "Well, what's the news, Brian?"

Brian slid his official detective, spiral notebook from his pocket. He took a deep breath, pulled up his jeans, and started. "I lost them for a while, but then I remembered they wanted to take the horse and wagon tour. I caught up with them there. After that I trailed them to their car in the parking lot. And that's when I noticed it."

"The license plate," said Sammy.

"What?" said Brian.

"That's when you noticed the license plate."

"I know that," replied Brian, adding, "but the plate—"

"It wasn't from the state of Ohio," said Sammy. Brian's open mouth pointed at Sammy. "How did you know that?" he asked.

"Our friend, Glen Rock, mentioned about '*coming up* here, *coming up* this way.' If you're from Ohio, you don't *come up* to Pennsylvania. He has to be from a southern state."

"Yeah, Virginia," said Brian, reluctantly. He was mad at himself for not picking up on the clue. Then he added, "What did you find out? Is it Mr. Parker's house? Was that his son Adam?"

"No, a family by the name of Johnson lives there."

"But . . . Groff," said Brian.

"Probably a grandson. Hey, a lot of nine-year-old boys live in this area. Hundreds of people work here in the Village. And some of them lived here for a couple months." Sammy hesitated. "Finding Charles Parker is not going to be easy. It's going to take a lot of investigation and problem solving. So let's continue where we left off."

The duo stopped for a late lunch then visited several more shops. They had to remember, their cover was the kidnapped frog. So they asked questions directed at the kidnapping. "When was the last time you were in the business office? When was the last time you saw the frog? Did anyone ask or talk about the frog before it was taken? Did you take the frog?"

Woven in among the inquiries were casual questions. Questions related to Charles Parker, the hidden witness. The answers to these questions were considered potential clues for the Parker case. "How long have you run this shop? Do you have any new employees? How old are they? Any hired within the last year? Who does your bookkeeping?"

Every shop owner and employee was aware that the frog had been kidnapped but said they knew nothing more about it. The topic initiated a lot of laughs and a few, "Are you boys for real?" With every shop they visited, however, the determined detectives learned where Charles Parker *was not.*

The last stop of the day was The Deerskin Leather shop. The owner was Jim Burnley, a son of Pat Burnley. Jim was amused at the questions asked about the frog's disappearance. He told the boys about Robert Efford who he hired earlier that year. Robert Efford was about thirty years old, short, and quite humorous. He had a truck with Florida license plates.

Jim Burnley also mentioned that a man had been in his shop that day asking questions about recently hired employees. He said the stranger gave him an uneasy feeling so he broke off the conversation.

Sammy made some notes including a description of the man. When the young detectives left the shop, they were optimistic but tired and ready to go home.

The tall man watched as the teen detectives mounted their bikes, exited the Village, and headed back to Bird-in-Hand. He smiled. The young detectives had been under his scrutiny all day. Soon the boys would know what they needed to know. What he wanted them to know.

Yes, everything was going as planned. Even the figure watching him from the bench was to be part of his plan. And now it was time to get the bench warmer's full attention. He withdrew the wrinkled photo from his pocket. The picture of Sammy Wilson and Brian Helm. He didn't need it anymore; he knew the boys well. Tearing the photo in half, he let the two pieces tumble to the ground. He turned and headed for the Kettle House Restaurant which was nearby.

While he skimmed the outside posted menu, his peripheral vision saw the man leave the bench and stroll over and pick up the torn photo pieces. He beamed. The operation was proceeding as designed. Having made his selection from the outside menu, he entered the restaurant. Confidence oozed from his body as his hand swept back over his bald head.

With the pieces of photo in hand, the man returned to the bench. His years of entanglement with the law told him that the tall, bald man with a mustache was trouble. He was either a cop or a fed. Yeah, maybe even a federal marshal, he thought to himself. Had the police gotten word that he had arrived to deal with Charles Parker?

He looked again at the torn photograph he had scooped from the ground. Yes, these were the two boys who just rode away on their bikes—the boys he had been following. Earlier he had seen them in several shops. They were asking questions about a frog. When they began inquiring about new employees hired within the last year, and about the bookkeeping, they became his target.

Asking his own questions, he learned the teenagers were Sammy Wilson and Brian Helm, famous local crime fighters. His face hardened. His muscles flexed. He realized he had competition.

He glanced to his right in time to see the neatly dressed bald man enter the restaurant. Why did the law have a snapshot of the boys? he wondered. Why was he tailing them? Are the boys getting that close to Charles Parker? He looked past the restaurant to the Grande-Place, Music Boxes and the tall oak tree in front. His eyes followed the branch that was only a step away from the balcony. A cunning smile graced his evil face. If his after-hours visit tonight was not successful, he would get Sammy and Brian to lead him to Parker.

CHAPTER EIGHT

Brian bounded up the wooden steps that led to Sammy's bedroom. "What's all the excitement about?" he asked.

Sammy, who was sitting behind his desk, had phoned Brian to tell him to show up early for their seven o'clock brainstorming session. Two important developments had occurred. "Come here. Look at this. It seems I got a special delivery on my e-mail from someone named Fedwell."

Breathing heavily, Brian hurried around the desk and stared at the monitor.

"I'm taking a chance, but tell the police someone knows that Charles Parker is in Kitchen Kettle Village. They'll find him. You can bet on that. Please get Parker out of the Village before his luck runs out."

"Somebody wants us to tell the police that Parker's cover is blown," said Brian. "Why us? Whoever sent this message should tell the police, not us."

Sammy looked again at the header information. "Brian, you hit the nail right on the head. I've been sitting here thinking about that. The e-mail address has the name Fedwell and the time it was sent. Now why wouldn't this Fedwell inform the police himself? And evidently our mystery e-mailer doesn't know that the authorities are already aware of it."

Brian retreated to his official spot at the foot of the bed. He lay back and glanced at the ceiling. Nothing moved. No black spots were roaming the area. He sighed. He missed Larry, his spider friend. He closed his eyes and thought about what it would be like to be a spider. Then he thought about a spider being a man, and a man being a spider. Then . . .

"I have it all figured out," said Brian, still focused on the ceiling. "The reason the person couldn't warn the police himself is because he isn't himself."

Sammy's right eye closed, his cheek wrinkled, and his mouth twisted to the side, developing a puzzled expression. "Did I hear what I just heard?" asked Sammy.

"Yeah, I reckon ya did, pardner," answered Brian in a western drawl.

His friend's attempt at western dialog told Sammy that Brian was venturing into the outer limits of brainstorming.

"I can't wait to hear this," said Sammy. "If the person isn't himself, then who is he?"

"A frog," answered Brian.

"A frog?" repeated Sammy.

"Sure. Don't you think it's strange that the creep frog shows up at Kitchen Kettle Village at the same time Charles Parker is placed here?"

"I don't recall—" started Sammy, shaking his head.

"Hey, trust me," said Brian, lifting his head. "When Charles Parker was changed into the frog, that's when the frog turned creepy. And," he said before Sammy could interrupt, "don't you think it odd that Marshal Springer knew we were going to meet Harry Clover about the kidnapped frog? Mr. Springer definitely has a connection to the frog."

Sammy's return look told Brian that his allotted speaking time on this subject was limited.

Brian hurried. "And when the marshals found out that Mack Roni was headed this way, the frog disappears. Kidnapped. Period. End of my brilliant deduction."

Sammy took a moment to assemble and digest Brian's "man to frog" theory. "Are you suggesting, Brian, that Marshal Springer put a curse on Charles Parker and changed him into a frog in order to hide him at the Village?"

Brian was back gazing at the ceiling. "Hey, can you think of a better way to change someone's identity and appearance? That's why Marshall Springer was so sure we wouldn't be able to find Charles Parker. He knew we would never suspect a frog. When this whole mess is over, Marshal Springer will cancel the curse and," Brian raised his hands into the air, "ta da, our relocated witness will reappear."

"Then you know who kidnapped the frog. *Right, Brian?*" said Sammy sarcastically.

"Oh, sure. Absolutely. Without question. It's elementary, my dear Holmes."

"Well?" asked Sammy, breaking the silence that followed. "Who done it?"

"It was . . . It was . . ." Brian sat up and grinned. "It was Mr. Parker's son. He wanted his daddy back."

Sammy rolled his eyes and shook his head. He looked again at the monitor. "In this fairy tale of yours, are you saying the frog, alias Charles Parker, sent us this e-mail after he found out that someone was coming to the Village to eat frog legs?"

"Hey, nicely put," said Brian as he sat up on the bed. "I like that."

"Yeah, right. Now let's return to the real world," said Sammy. "The other thing we need to discuss is Justin Groff and the Johnson house."

Brian frowned, his legs dangling over the edge of the bed. "I thought you gave up on that."

Sammy left his desk and stood by the window. "I almost did, but then I decided to check with Joyce Myers."

Anticipation was evident in Brian's voice as he glanced at the empty rocking chair and asked, "Is she going to help us with this case?"

"Why? Do you think we need help?"

"Well . . . no. But I bet she'd see the connection between the frog and Charles Parker . . . unlike someone else in this room."

Before Brian rattled on, Sammy said, "I don't know if we'll need Joyce's help or not. What I really wanted was to talk with her father."

Brian joined his friend at the window. This gave him time to make a connection between Mr. Myers and the case. "Ah, Joyce's father is in the real estate business. You asked him to check on any houses purchased within the last year." Brian puckered his lips. "Hmm, bought by a couple with a nine-year-old boy. Right, Sammy?"

"Yes, he is going to check on that, too. But I wanted information on Fred and Agnes Johnson and their house." Sammy produced an unexpected grin.

"Well, what? What?" asked Brian.

"It seems that the Johnsons moved in with their daughter and son-in-law and rented their house to the Groffs. A man, his wife, and Justin, a nine-year-old." At this point, Sammy lost his smile and frowned.

"What's wrong with that?" asked Brian. "That's great! Isn't it?"

"But here's the puzzling part. The house was rented for only two months, *starting last week.*"

"Why rent your house out for only two months?" added Brian. "That's crazy."

Sammy pointed his finger at his bed. "Let's bat that idea around for a while."

Brian was deep in thought by the time the bed creaked and he was again concentrating on the ceiling above. Sammy brushed his straight dark hair back from his blue eyes and realigned his chair to face away from the computer. From the new position he could see his buddy and the wall containing the bulletin board.

"Let's start with the notion that the Groffs are *not* Mr. Parker and his family," suggested Sammy. "Why would the Groffs rent the Johnsons' house for only two months?"

"Okay," said Brian, "the Groffs are friends or relatives of the Johnsons. They needed a place to stay until they found a house of their own. Mr. Johnson gave them two months to buy a house."

"Good," said Sammy as he reached for some paper and a pen and made some notes.

Brian continued as if reading from a list on the ceiling. "The Johnsons need extra money, so they rented the house to tourists for two months."

"Hey, you're on a roll," said Sammy.

"The Johnsons . . . The Johnsons . . ." said Brian, trying to keep the momentum going. "The Johnsons need work done inside the house. Mrs. Johnson couldn't stand the noise and dust so they moved until the work is done." Brian smiled at the ceiling.

"So the Johnsons rented their house to a workman named Groff with a nine-year-old son?" asked Sammy.

"Hey, all of my delicate thoughts can't be gems. I'm only human you know."

"Oh, really? I thought you were Brian Helm, Super Detective, champion of the people, faster than a speeding bullet."

"True," said Brian, "but it's my mouth that's faster than a speeding bullet. My brain's a little slower."

A weak laugh tumbled from Sammy then stopped. "Okay, the Johnsons. Now, let's assume the Groffs *are* Charles Parker and his family. Why would the Johnsons rent their house to the Parkers for only two months?"

"The marshals want to keep moving the Parkers from place to place," said Brian. "You know, two months here, two months there."

"Seems the moving would draw attention to them," added Sammy. "It's the opposite of what they really want." Having said that, Sammy wanted to start with a fact. "We know the Parkers have been in the Village for many months. Now all of a sudden they are uprooted and made to live in the Johnsons' house for two months. Something's wrong here."

"Okay, so maybe they aren't the Parkers, but let's pretend . . ." started Brian.

Sammy's arms sprung up into the air. "Oh, Brian, you are a genius! Why didn't I see it before?" He quickly made notes on the paper.

"I'm glad somebody recognizes my brilliance." But Brian's wide, artificial grin collapsed into a frown. "See what?" he asked, jumping up from the bed. "What do you see?"

"I see it's a mistake. If I'm right, they made a big mistake."

"What mistake?"

Sammy stood and went straight to the bulletin board. He focused on a news article with a familiar headline. "Bird-in-Hand's two super sleuths do it again. Sammy Wilson and Brian Helm solve the case of Jonathan's journal." He didn't need to read the rest of it; he and Brian had lived it.

"What big mistake did they make?" repeated Brian.

Sammy looked at his friend. "Their mistake was, they only needed to rent the house for *one* month."

CHAPTER NINE

All was not well at the Grande-Place the next morning. You couldn't tell from the outside, but inside the shop, the evidence declared it a break-in. The broken glass on the floor beneath the one window showed the port of entry. The intruder had climbed the oak tree, stepped over onto the balcony, and smashed his way in through the window.

The burglar was experienced enough to know he had about five minutes to get in and out. The elaborate alarm security system placed around the Village would alert the security. They would call to verify it as a real break-in and then respond. Arrival time—five minutes.

The splintered wood of the door frame indicated that the office door had been forced open. The intruder had no time to play around with the lock. File folders were scattered about the desk. Two were missing. One listed employee home addresses and phone numbers. The other

contained employment information on Dale Frey—
Piano Doctor.

Five minutes was all the hoodlum needed
to grab the files. He knew what he was after, and
he knew where it was.

Who would dare break in and shatter the
innocents of Kitchen Kettle Village? wondered Al
Lowrey. He picked up the large pieces from among
the cluster of glass. His brush coaxed the smaller
pieces onto the dust pan. Luckily only one glass
pane was broken.

Linda Lowrey's displays were not disturbed.
Al was pleased. It was strange, though, that none
of the music boxes were taken or even moved.
The police, too, were surprised that the files were
the only things stolen.

Normally at this hour of the morning Todd,
Al's son, would be placing music box movements
into figurines. But not this morning. Zulu needed
his attention. Zulu was a twelve-year-old African
gray parrot. Her cage hung from the ceiling above
Todd's work area.

Poor Zulu. The parrot was traumatized by
the unexpected early morning break-in. Even
though Todd was trying his best to calm Zulu's
fears, the parrot talked on and on, spitting out
new sounds. These were added to her already 300-
word and -sound vocabulary.

Todd, twenty-three, short, with brown hair
parted in the middle, was amazed at Zulu's new
mutterings. Dispersed throughout the parrot's

words and sound effects were the sounds of glass breaking and the whistling of the tune Yankee Doodle. Well, anyway, it sounded like Yankee Doodle.

The whistling fascinated Sammy as he entered the shop. The young detective had decided it would be a better use of time if Brian and he split up to investigate the remaining shops. First on Sammy's list was the Grande-Place. If Sammy's inference about the Groffs and the house was correct, more clues had to be collected, and quickly. When he arrived at the Village and heard the Grande-Place had been broken into, that became his first investigation.

The whistling came from the corner of the shop. People had gathered, listening. Was it a music box? Sammy wondered. He glanced up. No, it was a bird, a gray bird with a red tail.

Sammy remembered from his visit to this shop last year that a parrot occupied a cage in the corner. But the parrot was stubborn. She hardly ever made a sound when you wanted her to, but now she was doing a non-stop musical.

As Sammy approached, Todd was explaining to the folks about the many sounds that Zulu imitated. "She only has to hear the sound once and she remembers it," said Todd. "Sometimes we hear the phone ringing. When we answer it, no one's there. It's Zulu, playing a joke by imitating the sound of a ringing phone." He added, "The sounds of glass breaking and the whistle are sounds I've never heard her make before. We had someone break into our shop last night. A glass pane was broken. I think Zulu is repeating that sound." Todd shrugged. "And it's possible the intruder was whistling Yankee Doodle."

Sammy frowned. Would a person breaking into a shop whistle? he wondered. He grinned as the answer occurred. People do whistle in the dark when they're afraid. He found himself humming the catchy tune as he searched for the owner of the shop. He had information to collect and time was short.

Brian entered heaven. It was first on his list. Garrahy's Fudge Kitchen. He had heard they offered free samples of their delicious fudge varieties.

Inside, a white plastic fence separated the customers from the three solid marble tables. Debby, a woman in her thirties with short brown curly hair, was working a slab of warm fudge on one of the tables. She used a mixing paddle to beat the fudge, pushing it the full length of the marble table.

Brian could see the fudge was still a warm liquid as the young woman ran the paddle along the side of the flowing candy. She constantly flipped the rich, soft candy over into itself, mixing and stirring. This action gave it a smooth, creamy texture.

Then without warning, as Debby was working the paddle, some warm fudge flew off the table and landed on Brian's shirt. Brian looked down and smiled. "Hey, it's true. You really do give free samples here. But your method of delivery needs work."

Debby apologized and offered to clean his shirt. But Brian refused. He had his own delicious way to remove the fudge.

As his blood sugar count increased, Brian asked the necessary questions about the kidnapped frog. He zeroed in with questions about Parker. Debby supplied no useful information. When Brian left "fudge heaven," his notes were few. The only lasting impression was the brown stain on his shirt.

The next stop on Brian's list was Top Brass, a shop with things made of brass. But someone had other ideas. In the walkway between two shops, a figure beckoned for Brian to come his way.

"Oh, no, not another one," said Brian to himself. This time the teenager hesitated before plunging ahead into the unknown. He didn't want a repeat of yesterday's escapade.

"Hi, Brian. It's okay. I was told to check in with you," said the friendly stranger.

Brian took several steps closer. There was something familiar about this man. Do all federal marshals give off the same wave vibrations? he wondered. He noted the many tourists passing by. "Who told you to check on me? Sammy?" asked Brian.

"No. You know. Tall and bald," replied the man secretively.

"Oh, Marshal Springer," said Brian, advancing toward the stranger.

The man nodded. "Yeah, well, we call him 'baldy,' but not to his face of course."

"You must be a marshal, too," said Brian.

The man nodded again. "So, you haven't found him yet, have you?"

The smirk and tone of voice did not please Brian. He stood tall and produced his secret agent voice. "We definitely do know where Charles Parker is."

The man's face lit up. "Sh, not so loud. We don't want this information to fall into the wrong hands. Do we?"

Brian hunched his shoulders and place his hand over his mouth. "Oops, sorry," said Brian, losing his secret agent image.

"Where is he?" asked the man, whispering.

"The chief . . . I mean Sammy and I are getting our reports ready. You'll hear from us shortly," was all Brian could manage to say.

"But you do know where Charles Parker is?"

Brian swallowed hard. He couldn't admit the truth now. It was too late. "Yep, we sure do," he heard himself say.

"Great then, I'll see you later."

Brian watched as the man walked past him and vanished into the crowd. The whistled melody followed the mysterious individual.

Brian recognized the tune.
Yankee Doodle.

CHAPTER TEN

S
ammy listened as Brian trudged up the stairway, his hands sliding along the wall. Sammy found it a challenge as well as a necessity to gage his friend's mood in advance. Tonight especially, Sammy needed his buddy to be in top form for brainstorming.

The puzzle pieces that Sammy had managed to put together so far did not produce a pretty picture. The case was biting back and Sammy was feeling the sting. He hoped he was wrong, but the clues collected so far told him he was probably on target. What he didn't appreciate was that Brian and he were in the bull's-eye. What he heard coming up the steps only added to his frustration.

Without saying a word, Brian collapsed on the bed, flopped back, and welcomed the ceiling's willingness to absorb his troubles.

"What's wrong, Brian?"

Brian mumbled something. The understandable part was, " . . . to keep my mouth shut."

"What?" asked Sammy.

"Oh, nothing."

Brian was feeling guilty. Earlier, riding home from the Village, the boys had discussed the results of their interviews at the various shops. And while Brian told of his humorous adventure at the Fudge Kitchen, he didn't see any harm in "forgetting" to tell Sammy about his meeting with the "marshal."   .

Experience told Sammy that if he didn't press the issue, his friend would ultimately share his problem. And then Brian would expect him to take the problem and change it into a creative learning experience.

Sammy glanced again at the printout that lay on his desk. "Brian, if you were put into the Witness Relocation Program and moved to another state, what would you take with you?"

A voice arose from the bed. "My coin collection."

Sammy saw the need for a direct example. "Let me revamp the question. If you were Charles Parker and put into the program and shipped off to another state, what would you to take with you?"

"My wife and son."

"What else?"

"Any pets I might have," answered Brian mechanically, sounding like a robot.

Sammy smiled. He realized Brian was trying to sound like a computer, spitting out the answers.

"What else?"

Brian tilted his head up and looked at Sammy. "Hey, I like this game." And then converting back to the ceiling and his computerized voice said, "I would take . . . my clothing."

"What else?"

"My car," he continued in his robotic voice. Sammy paused. "No. Your car would be registered under your real name. They would have to get you a new car using your new name."

Brian frowned and in a monotone said, "Sorry boss, I developed a glitch."

"What else would you take, *Brian*?" asked Sammy, using his get-back-to-business tone.

"My computer."

Sammy hadn't considered that as a possibility before. After pausing for thought, his fingers hit the keys. The computer played its musical wake-up call and the monitor awoke. When the computer booted up and was fully dressed, Sammy clicked on an icon. As the program opened up, Sammy saw what he needed. He made a note on his pad and circled it.

"Okay, what else?"

Still maintaining a mechanical intonation, Brian continued. "My workshop tools. Remember, according to the article, he built the flower room for his wife."

"Good," said Sammy. "What else?"

"Ah, er, . . . my furniture."

"Right!" said Sammy. "Brian, look at this."

The bed rocked and his legs shot him into the air. Both Sammy and Brian were surprised that he landed on his feet.

"What? You never saw my gymnastic skills before?" asked Brian, still wondering how he did that.

"Take a look at this and tell me what you see."

"It's the copy of the article about Lois Parker, Chuck's wife."

"Who?" asked Sammy.

"You know. Chuck. That's a nickname for Charles. My Uncle Charles is called Chuck."

"I know that," said Sammy. "It was just odd, hearing you call Mr. Parker that."

"Well, by now, I feel I know him. He seems like an old friend," answered Brian.

"What else do you see in this picture besides *Chucky's* wife?" asked Sammy.

"Flowers, the window, the picture on the back wall, part of a piano, the chair that she's sitting . . . Furniture!" yelled Brian.

"Bingo," said Sammy. "Now, Brian, old friend, if you just happen to visit the Johnsons' house tomorrow and you're invited inside, you might see some of this furniture."

"Yeah, *if* I can get inside, and *if* the Groffs are really Charles Parker and his family."

"Brian, I know by tomorrow morning, you'll have a plan to get yourself inside that house. Legally, that is."

Sammy's reassuring blue eyes granted Brian the nerve to accept the challenge.

Sammy's finger came to rest on the black silhouette protruding partly from the edge of the picture. "You're right about this being a piano. Someone in the family plays it."

"Maybe they all play the piano," said Brian, grinning, feeling the satisfaction of being called right by Sammy.

"Remember I told you about the trouble at Grande-Place? Well, Al Lowrey said the day before, a man had asked him if he had hired anyone in the last year. When Al mentioned he had hired a man to fix pianos, the man asked for his address. He said he was trying to locate an old friend."

"So when Al refused to supply the address," said Brian, "the man broke in and helped himself to the information."

"I believe Mack Roni has arrived. And like us, he's following leads to locate Charles Parker."

"Yeah, it sure sounds like it," said Brian.

"Speaking of sounds," said Sammy. "I met Todd, Al's son, and finally got to hear that parrot talk."

"What parrot?" asked Brian.

"At the Grande-Place. The African gray parrot with the red tail. Zulu. You know. She's in the cage, hanging in the corner."

"Hey, don't let them fool you," said Brian. "That parrot can't talk. It's Todd. He makes the sounds."

"I heard it, today, Brian. That bird talked."

Brian shook his head. "Don't you think it's strange that Zulu's cage is right above where Todd works. And you remember the last time we were there the parrot didn't talk until we walked away. It's definitely Todd doing the talking."

"Today I was three feet away, facing the bird—and facing Todd. And they were both talking at the same time. Not only that, but Zulu was whistling Yankee Doodle."

Brian was not going to give up easily. "Did you ever see a ventriloquist drink water and at the same time . . ." Brian's face turned white. "Yankee Doodle?"

"Yeah, they think the person who broke in last night whistled that tune. Zulu repeated it. They said she can remember and mimic any sound."

"Are you sure the song was Yankee Doodle?"

Sammy looked at Brian. "Well, it was close enough to be a ripoff. Something wrong? You don't look well."

The bed creaked and sagged and Brian was once more facing a blank ceiling. He lay still for a moment. Then with his fingers tightly clenched, he pounded the mattress. "I'm dumb, dumb, dumb!" he yelled.

"What happened?" asked Sammy as he came to the bed and glanced down.

"Oh, I'm dumb. That's all."

Sammy returned to his desk, pushed the papers aside, and sat on the top. He looked down at the floor and waited.

"The guy told me he was a marshal," Brian finally said. "He said Marshal Springer told him to check on us. You know, to see if we had found Charles Parker."

Sammy remained still and made no reply.

"I . . . I . . . I told him we . . . might know where Mr. Parker is."

Sammy said nothing.

Brian raised his head to check if Sammy was still in the room. Satisfied, his head fell back and his eyes rested on the ceiling. "But I didn't say where he was. I said we would disclose it in our report."

Sammy said nothing.

"Well, why don't you say something? What are you waiting for?" Brian bellowed at the ceiling.

Sammy's head sprang up. "I'm waiting for the *dumb* part."

"When the guy walked away, he whistled."

Sammy waited.

Brian sat up and looked his friend in the eye. "He whistled Yankee Doodle."

Now it was Sammy's turn. "The guy didn't show you a shield or identification, did he?"

Brian tapped his feet on the floor. "No."

"And you told him we *knew* where the Parkers were."

"Yeah," said Brian nodding. "My big mouth."

The two boys compared descriptions of the two men involved and decided that it had to be the same man. But was it Mack Roni?

"If it's the same man," said Brian, "why does he whistle Yankee Doodle all the time?"

Sammy raised his arms into the air. "Maybe it's his favorite song."

"I think it's a dumb song," said Brian. "The words don't make sense. He put a feather in his cap and called it macaroni. Now that's . . . macaroni? Hey, Mack Roni. The man *is* Mack Roni."

"You may have something there, Brian," said Sammy, sliding off the desk. "He got the nickname Mack Roni because he always whistles Yankee Doodle."

"But he's a gangster," said Brian. "What do you suppose he'll do now that he thinks we know where the Parkers are?" asked Brian. Not waiting for an answer, he added dramatically, "Hey, he might grab us. Torture us. Make us tell where the Parkers are."

"And what are you going to tell him when the pain gets too unbearable?"

"The way things are going I'll spill the beans and say, 'They live in the white house on Main Street.' "

"Good," replied Sammy, much to Brian's surprise.

"Good? What's good about it? You think the Parkers aren't there?"

Sammy grinned and went to the window. "I *know* the Parkers aren't there."

"Then why am I going to the house tomorrow to check on the furniture?"

"Because that's part of the plan," replied Sammy.

"What plan?"

Sammy shook his head. "I'm not exactly sure. It's best you don't know."

"Oh, really?" said Brian. He walked out the door and started down the steps. "Well, I'm going home to practice for my house-warming party tomorrow."

"Yeah? What's your plan?" Sammy yelled after him.

Brian's feet danced down the steps. "It's best you don't know, Sammy. It's best you don't know."

CHAPTER ELEVEN

With bicycles in hand, the teenage detectives walked the rest of the way. At nine o'clock in the morning, the ride to Kitchen Kettle Village was uneventful. Most places of business opened at ten o'clock, so it was the calm before the storm—of tourists. Traffic was light, the sky promised a rainless day, and the Village awaited its share of the tourist trade.

The boys stopped and took cover behind a parked car. They were across the street and a half block away from the white house. From there they would oversee their operation. Or rather, Brian's operation.

"That's the house," said Sammy, pointing to the one between the two brick houses.

"Looks peaceful enough," said Brian. "Maybe we're too early."

"No, go ahead." said Sammy. "Surprise me. Let's see this open-house party you've planned."

Brian was ready to push off on his bike when Sammy stopped him. "Hold it! Look, at the back of the house."

A man was running from the rear of the white house to the front lawn of the brick house. He hurried along as he dashed for the road, heading in the direction of the Village.

"Sammy, that looks like Glen Rock," exclaimed Brian, staying low behind the car.

"That's him all right," confirmed Sammy. "I wonder where his wife and son are?"

"Oh, my gosh, what if he harmed the Parkers."

The fleeing man soon passed them on the other side of the road. The deep-set eyes and bushy eyebrows forged ahead. No doubt about it, the man was Glen Rock. What was he doing here? And where did this piece of the puzzle fit in? wondered Sammy. He would worry about that later. It was important now for Brian to enter the house.

"Go, Brian, go," said Sammy pushing the bike, but not really knowing Brian's plan of attack. Regardless of his pal's faults, Brian could at times be amazing. Sammy was praying this would be one of those times.

Brian aimed his bike toward the house. After crossing the road, the bike settled on a path across the front lawn. Suddenly the bike stopped. The rear wheel lifted from the ground, throwing Brian forward and twisting the handle bars. Brian flipped off to the side and slid on the grass—until he met the tree. Only his mother would be concerned about the grass stains.

Being accustomed to his buddy's theatrics, Sammy didn't know whether to laugh or rush to Brian's aid. Was this his friend's plan, or was it one of Brian's blunders?

Before Sammy could react, Brian got up, hobbled around the tree, across the lawn, and knocked at the door.

Sammy shook his head and watched as the door opened and a man appeared. The two spoke for a while and then Brian vanished behind the closed door. Sammy took a deep breath and relaxed against the car. Gradually his heartbeat returned to normal. At least two people were alive in the house. But for how long?

Brian was all smiles as he pushed his deformed bike up the road. When he was across from the car and without turning his head, Brian said, "He's watching out the window. Stay where you are for a while." Brian continued to limp as he coaxed his disabled bike in the direction of the Village.

Sammy was encouraged by Brian's smile. But the rest of Brian deserved pity. Sammy waited until the window curtain fell back into place before he mounted his bike and followed his friend.

Tourists were accumulating as Sammy caught up with Brian near the parking lot. Cars, campers, and buses were claiming their spaces in the large parking area. The young detectives propped their bikes against a tree and chained them together.

The excited teen couldn't wait to tell his buddy the good news. "It's Charles Parker, all right. You can tell it's him."

Sammy was skeptical. "You mean the man who let you into the house? That was Charles Parker?"

"No doubt about it," said Brian. "He looked just like him. And Sammy, guess what? I think he has a gun. I saw a holster strapped under his arm."

"Hmm," said Sammy. "How about the furniture? Did you see any of it?"

"No, I didn't. I looked for the chair, for the piano, and for the picture. I was in the living room and went to the dining room to use the phone." Brian produced a wide grin and winked. "I had to call my mother to tell her about the accident, and that I would be late getting home."

"Who else was in the house?" asked Sammy.

"I didn't see anyone," said Brian. "But I thought I heard some sounds coming from a bedroom." Brian pulled on Sammy's arm. "Okay, so let's go phone Marshal Springer and tell him we found Charles Parker."

"Not just yet," said Sammy.

"But if we found him, that means Mack Roni can, too."

"Did you forget about Glen Rock?" asked Sammy. "What was he doing at the house?"

Brian pointed a finger into the air. "Ah, back at the house, I asked about that. He said he had no visitors. He said the guy was probably taking a shortcut through his back yard."

If Sammy was right, that clinched it. He didn't want to believe it, but all the clues pointed to one conclusion. While he understood the reasoning behind it, he didn't like the deception.

He observed the people nearby. Was anyone listening? Were they being watched? Earlier he was careful that Brian and he were not followed to the house. But now . . . Kitchen Kettle Village was coming alive. People were everywhere.

From the corner of his eye, Sammy saw the swift action of a man coming at them. Nearer. A brick in his raised hand. A natural reflex caused both Sammy and Brian to draw back, ready to defend themselves.

"You boys should get one of these made," said Harry Clover. He held the brick so they could read the engraving on it.

"What is it?" asked Brian as he caught his breath and noted someone's name and hometown.

"You buy a brick, have your name engraved on it, and it becomes part of the walkway over there. Part of the money goes to the Lancaster Farmland Trust. They work to preserve our farmland."

"You make a good salesman," said Sammy. "It sounds like a good idea."

Brian was wondering if a likeness of himself could be engraved on the brick.

"Have you figured out where the frog is?" asked Harry.

"No, but we're shaking people up," said Brian. "The guilty person will crack soon and then we'll have the frog back."

"You even sound like real detectives," said Harry. He regretted using the word real when he saw the look on the boys' faces. "I'm sorry . . . It's just . . . I'd like to get the frog back. Mrs. Burnley is developing the new catalog for the Village and needs the frog and *him* for photographs." Harry was pointing to a tall, completely covered, brown creature surrounded by a group of excited children.

The "him" was Yummy. Yummy was the Gingerbread Man, the Village mascot. Everyday throughout the summer, Yummy appeared for the enjoyment of the visitors. He didn't talk, but he did giggle a lot.

Sammy did some calculating. "We'll have the frog for you within two days."

Brian wanted to say something but not in front of the client.

"Great!" said Harry. Then looking at the brick and turning away, he added, "Hey, I have to plant this back in the walkway. See you."

Sammy pointed to the Gingerbread Man and said to Brian, "He should chuck that hot, brown costume and get a cooler white one."

"What?" asked Harry who was not quite out of hearing range.

"I said your Gingerbread Man should wear a lighter costume," exclaimed Sammy.

"Yeah, maybe he should be Snow White," said Harry, continuing the route to the walkway. He was laughing so much he almost dropped the engraved brick.

When Harry was out of hearing distance, Brian asked, "How are we going to get the kidnapper to return the frog in two days?"

"Follow me and I'll tell you." Sammy headed for The Smokehouse Shop. "I'm going to visit the shops and tell everyone that Mrs. Burnley needs the frog for the new catalog. And I'll tell them how to return it without anybody knowing who . . ."

A recognizable blur caused Sammy to shift gears and stop. The action on the other side of the window fascinated the young detective. The sign outside said Kettle House Restaurant. The teenager sitting inside told Sammy that a snack was in order.

Sammy pointed to the window. "Come on, Brian, we're hungry."

Brian didn't argue about the being hungry part, but he did squint in through the window to see what brought on the sudden appetite.

The boy sitting at the table was Glen Rock, Junior. In front of him was a pile of lottery tickets.

Brian smiled. "Donuts, here I come."

The boys set their trays down on a table next to Glen Junior. The intensity of his concentration kept Junior from noticing the detectives, or anyone for that matter. His actions were predictable. He tore a ticket from the large roll, scratched it with a coin, grimaced, and then tossed it on the large loser's pile. The winner's pile was hardly noticeable. In fact, it was hardly a pile at all.

Brian swallowed some milk to wash down his mouthful of donut. Before he stuck the other half of the donut into his mouth, he said, "You must have spent all of your vacation money to buy those tickets."

"And then some," replied Glen Junior without interrupting his quest for wealth.

"We saw your father this morning," said Sammy and waited for a reaction.

Junior flipped a ticket at the loser's pile and looked over. "Hi. Yeah, I'm waiting for him myself. You still working your case?" he asked without missing the rhythm of rip, scratch, frown, and toss—rip, scratch, frown, and toss—rip, scratch, frown, and toss.

"No, no case," said Sammy. "We're kind of on vacation."

"But you work with the police, don't you?"

Sammy nodded his head and asked, "Does your father work with police in his line of work?"

Glen Junior showed no mercy as he ripped the last two tickets apart. "Twenty-four hours a day. Hey, a word of advice." He scrapped the quarter across the ticket. "Don't stay in the detective game. It will eat you up. My dad's hardly ever home." He frowned and added the ticket to the large heap.

Sammy pressed his lips together and squinted as the quarter dug into the last ticket and made it almost unreadable. "I know what you're saying," said Sammy. "My parents are busy, too. But at least we are together in the morning, at meal time, and most evenings."

"I was hoping my dad would spend time with me on this vacation. But, as you see . . ." He flung the final ticket with such energy it toppled the cardboard mountain. "I can't win. I'm a loser," he said as he watched some worthless tickets slid and fall to the floor.

"I'll get those for you," said Brian as he rushed from his chair and around to the fallen pieces.

Glen Junior didn't seem to hear or react to Brian's remark. Instead, he gazed at the small stack of two-dollar and free-ticket winners. Laying the tickets side by side, he quickly calculated. His face produced a cynical smile. "I'm a winner after all. I won fourteen dollars."

Wanting to explain the reality of the situation to Junior, Sammy asked, "How many free tickets do you have?"

"Four," said Junior. "So you can say I won four dollars there."

"How much did those four 'winning' tickets cost you?" asked Sammy.

"Four . . . So I'm not winning anything. I'm just getting four more tickets—to prolong the agony."

"Right," said Sammy. "And how much did the five two-dollar tickets cost you?"

"Okay, I get it," said Junior. "So in all I won five dollars."

"How much did the losing tickets cost you in order for you to win those five dollars?"

Junior did some quick math. "Ninety-one dollars," he said with reluctance. "That's the story of my life. Even when I win, I lose."

Brian put the picked-up tickets on the table. "You still might win something if one of your signed, free tickets is picked in the drawing."

"There's no end to my losing, is there? Now I must somehow get my name and address in that little space on the back of the four tickets." He looked pleadingly at Sammy. "Do you have a pen I can use?"

Feeling sorry for the boy, Sammy slipped a pen from his pocket and replied, "Here, keep it. Come on, Brian, we should go."

Junior made no attempt to say thank you or to acknowledge their leaving. His task at hand was to hurriedly record his name and address in miniature.

Sammy took his time as he pushed the waste into the trash can and placed the empty tray with the others on top. A side glance revealed that Junior had finished writing. Sammy grabbed Brian's arm. "Brian, wait here. I'll be right back."

Sammy retraced his steps back to Junior's table. Words were said, and when Sammy returned, he was holding a lottery ticket. Sammy kept walking and Brian followed out the door.

"What's with the ticket?" asked Brian as he blinked at the sunlight.

"It's one of his free tickets. I gave him five dollars for it."

Brian took the scratched ticket and examined it. "You gave him five dollars for a ticket you trade in for *one* new ticket? You can buy *five* new tickets for five dollars." Brian turned the ticket over. "And his name's already written on it, in ink."

"Yeah, how about that?" said Sammy, smiling.

"But we already know his . . ." Brian examined the small writing. "Hey, he wrote Glen Dixon Junior, and gives an address in Virginia."

Sammy reclaimed the ticket from Brian. "He had to write his real name in order to qualify for any winnings."

"But you talked him into parting with one ticket for five dollars."

"Even he knows a bird in the hand is worth two in the bush."

Brian puckered his lips, snickered, and said, "I think I've heard that saying before. But why did his father lie about his name?"

"We'll know that when we find out who Glen Dixon really is. I have some things to do. You take that ticket to our friend, Detective Phillips, and see if he'll do a name check for us. We need all the clues we can get."

If you didn't know what to look for, you wouldn't have seen the deep-set eyes and bushy eyebrows peering out from inside the Jam and Relish Kitchen. With the aid of binoculars, those eyes had witnessed where Sammy had gotten the lottery ticket and the possible consequences the ticket could create.

The man turned from the window and glanced back through the displays of jellies and jams. His dark eyes settled on the stairway and followed it up to the business office. Then he thought about the frog.

CHAPTER TWELVE

The expensive blue set of wheels was parked but not empty. The car and its occupant rested under the two signs, Bird-in-Hand Junction and Bird-in-Hand Country Store. The man drummed his fingers on the steering wheel, while his lips whistled a happy tune. When he saw the teenager knock on the door and enter the house, he picked up his cell phone. Yankee Doodle was getting ready to go to town—but not yet. First, he had to get word to Vincent Bruno.

Brian was fifteen minutes early as he dashed up the steps to the bedroom. He was talking before he opened the door. "Sammy, I have good news for you, and I have surprising news for you. What do you want to hear first?"

His friend was sitting at the oak desk with his hands interlocked behind his head. The slight smile simmering on Sammy's face indicated he had anticipated Brian's positive outburst. "Tell me the good news first."

"The good news is, Detective Phillips got a printout on Glen Dixon from Virginia, alias, Glen Rock from Ohio. And on Glen Junior."

Brian said no more. He waited. He was teasing his buddy. But Sammy was waiting patiently. Finally, Brian couldn't stand it anymore. "Well, don't you want to hear the surprising news?"

"You mean that our friend, Glen Dixon, is a federal marshal?" said Sammy, making a well calculated guess.

Brian was about to sit on the bed, but Sammy's revelation changed his mind. "How did you know that? Ben Phillips called you. Didn't he? Yeah, that's it. He didn't trust me to deliver the good news. He had to do it himself. Right, Sammy?"

Sammy had done it again. In his attempt at honesty, he had hurt his friend's self-esteem. "Brian, I want you to take your official brainstorming position, look at the ceiling and tell me what you see."

Moaning and groaning, Brian did as he was told.

"I don't see anything on the ceiling," he said, after a quick scan.

"Right, Brian, there's nothing there. And what you just said. There's no truth to it. Detective Ben Phillips didn't tell me the surprising news. You did."

Brian's head raised from the bed. "I did?"

"Sure, the way you ran up the stairway, the enthusiasm and surprise in your voice, all told me what I had expected."

"You expected Glen Dixon to be a federal marshal?"

"He had to be, after we . . ."

"Bet you don't know about his son," said Brian, fighting to improve his reputation.

"No, that I don't. What's the scoop?"

"The scoop is, Glen Dixon Junior likes to gamble. He got in over his head with bookies in Virginia. The report says he was arrested after he used a gun to threaten a bookie's life. They found out later that the gun was a fake. His father . . ."

"SAMMY!" boomed a voice from downstairs. "PHONE!"

"Your father sure knows how to communicate," said Brian, resting his head back on the bed.

Sammy jumped from his chair. His actions showed the urgency and concern of the phone call. His expression showed he was not prepared for what he suspected. "I'll be right back," he said as he passed Brian.

What now? wondered Brian. He thought about the new turn of events. It made sense now why Glen Dixon was in the white house with Charles Parker and his family. Glen Dixon and Steve Springer must be working together, he thought. But why wasn't Marshal Dixon with Marshal Springer when Sammy and he were tested? It all was too much for Brian to think about. He would let Sammy do the thinking.

Sammy's speed up the steps was predictable to Brian. It was always the same regardless of the situation. Brian had a theory. When coming up the steps, Sammy was in his reasoning mode. So Brian came to the conclusion that his buddy's use of the steps was only to bring his thinking to a higher level.

"The phone call finally came," said Sammy. "You don't have to come with me. But I'm not sure when I'll be back."

Brian bounced up from the bed. "What was the phone call about?"

"It was from Charles Parker, our hidden witness. He wants to talk to us right away. We're to go to his house."

"Wow! A direct invitation. Great. So they know that we know . . . But how do they know that we know?"

"When the caller said to come to his place, he didn't give the address. Which means he's under the impression we know where he lives."

"Well, sure, after I was at the house today, he probably identified me from the picture that Marshal Springer has of us. They know we know so they invite us over. They want to celebrate our finding Charles Parker. I bet they have a surprise party ready for us."

"Brian, when I tried to pin him down about the address of his house, he wouldn't tell me. He just said I knew where it was."

"Hmm, strange. He should know his own address."

"That's, if it was Mr. Parker who called," said

Sammy. "That's why I don't think you should go. There could be trou . . ."

Brian flew out the door and down the steps. "Of course it's Mr. Parker. Come on. We can be there in twenty minutes. I don't want to be late for my own surprise party."

Lights were on inside the white house. But the outside porch lights were off. Curtains at the front window shivered as though someone had disturbed the air nearby.

The teenage detectives were breathing hard as they leaned their bikes against a tree. Sammy noticed the blue car that was parked a short distance away. It was the same car that followed them from Bird-in-Hand. Light reflecting off the windshield made it impossible to see the driver. But someone was watching them.

Sammy had mixed feeling about what he was about to do. Knocking on the door was the easy part. It was what would happen next that concerned him. The puzzle pieces he had put together presented a certain picture. But had he assembled them correctly? And what if he had not collected enough pieces of the puzzle to see the complete picture?

Brian was thinking how fortunate they had been to run into Charles Parker's son. How the son had led Sammy to this house. How Sammy had investigated the ownership of the house. How the Johnsons' had rented out the house for two months to the Parkers. It really was the Parkers because he, Brian, had personally recognized the man as Charles Parker. Brian was all smiles as Sammy and he walked to the door. The first question Brian was going to ask Mr. Parker after the celebration was over, was, Why did you rent this house for two months?

Sammy rang the doorbell.

No response.

Sammy pushed the button again.

The door opened.

"Hello, Mr. Parker," said Brian. "Here we are."

"And?" asked the man.

"But you called us and said to meet you here. You wanted . . ."

"Oh, yes, come in. Come in. Hurry!" The man leaned out, took a quick look around, and quickly closed the door.

It wasn't until the boys were inside that they became aware of the two men standing on either side of the doorway. The men were tall, muscular, and were not smiling. Nor were they wearing welcome signs.

Brian squirmed as he was seized by the man on the left.

Sammy, not fully understanding what was happening, was face to face with the man who strongly resembled Charles Parker. "Hi, Sammy," he said. "Sorry we have to do this, but . . . Take them to the basement."

The man on the right took Sammy by the shoulders and marched him into the kitchen. Brian was forced to followed, but under protest. "Hey, you guys have the wrong interpretation of surprise party," he screamed.

The man propelling Brian toward the basement door in the kitchen cranked out a small chuckle. "Take it easy. The surprise party is downstairs."

"Is that what it's all about?" asked Brian, who started to calm down considerably. "You're doing this to us because we found your precious Charles Parker. Boy, are you guys poor losers."

"Listen, *Shorty*, if you don't want to get hurt, you better get down these steps."

Sammy and the other man had already reached the bottom of the stairway.

"Brian, it's all right," said Sammy, who was already peering around the dimly lit family room.

Brian was red in the face. "And don't call me Shorty. Hey, okay, I may be short but can you do this?" Brian raised his hands to show the man something he was doing with his fingers. When the man bent over to see, Brian belted him with two fists to the face. The unexpected flurry of knuckles did nothing to the husky man except made him relax his grip on Brian's arm. Brian head-butted the man back against the door and took off across the kitchen to a bedroom. If he could get to a window . . .

A hand clamped across his mouth, an arm wrapped itself around his chest, pinning his arms to his body. His shoes left the floor two feet below. He was hauled over to the steps and handed back to his original captor. As he was lifted and carried down the stairway, he looked back. A woman in fatigues was smiling and waving at him. The door closed. She then silently and quickly returned to the bedroom.

Brian was in shock. Was the woman Lois Parker? he wondered. Was he just apprehended by the flower lady? The confused teenage detective was lugged across the family room and dumped on the sofa next to Sammy.

"Now, both of you, get behind the sofa."

There was no argument this time. Both boys did as they were told. But Brian was the first one to peer out over the sofa. Sammy followed.

One of the men stayed by the sofa, the other positioned himself in the corner to the rear of the steps.

Brian looked at his friend. "Do you think this is another test?"

"If it's a test for yelling and creating a ruckus, you won," said Sammy.

The teenager pointed to their guard. "Hey, I had to yell. See that thing in their ears? They're all hard of hearing."

Sammy was aware of the miniature earphones each man wore. In fact he had already heard bits and pieces of conversation that spilled out from them. He whispered to Brian, "That's part of their communication system. Listen."

". . . getting out of the car." The Ghost-like voice was coming from the guard's ear.

The boys inched closer.

" . . . coming this way."

"Subject going to back of house."

"He's looking in the window."

"He's moving to back door."

"Bingo, he found it unlocked."

"Okay, this is it. He's on his way in. Show time."

Then silence. Sammy and Brian looked at each other. The guard waved his hand at the boys and placed his finger to his lips. "Sh."

More silence. Only the hum of the central air fan could be heard.

Sammy could only imagine what was going on upstairs. A trap had been laid to lure someone into the house. It was only a matter of time before . . .

A muted scuffle, shouts, and a thud were heard.

And then . . . "Subject apprehended."

Good, thought Sammy, no shots were fired. At least he didn't hear any.

"You stay with them. I'm going up," said the voice from the corner.

The pair of legs going up the stairs met two pairs of legs coming down. "Are the boys down there."

"Yes, sir," came the reply.

Sammy and Brian stood up and shuffled around to the front of the sofa. They waited for heads to match the legs.

There were no surprises for either side. Sammy and Brian expected to see the two men. The two federal marshals expected to see the two aspiring detectives.

Marshal Dixon spoke to the marshal guarding the boys. "Bill, you can go up and help put the house back in shape for the Johnsons."

When the door closed and the four of them were alone, Dixon spoke again. "You boys know Marshal Steve Springer. And, because of my son and your clever detective work, you know who I am."

"If you know that," said Sammy, "your detecting and surveillance work isn't so bad itself."

"I got lucky," replied Dixon. "I happened to be at the right place at the right time."

Both marshals relaxed, smiled, and crossed the room to shake the boys' hands.

Brian wasn't buying this buddy, buddy stuff yet. While Sammy was shaking hands with both men, Brian said, "You used us in this sting operation of yours. You had Sammy and me lead Mack Roni right into your trap."

Marshal Springer spoke for the first time. "Remember when we had our last talk together? I said we couldn't do anything to Mack Roni until he committed a crime. Thanks to you, tonight, we caught him in the act. And he'll lead us right back to Vincent Bruno, the banker. His jail time will be extended considerably."

"But, you put our lives in danger," said Brian, "and the life of Charles Parker—if he still *is* alive upstairs."

Marshal Dixon yelled up the steps. "Hey, Marty, is Stan still there?"

A voice hollered back, "Yes sir, he is."

"Send him down," said Dixon.

A man descended the stairway and walked to Dixon's side. It was the same man who had answered the door both times. In the dim light he could pass for Charles Parker's twin. He was still clutching the book he was pretending to read when Mack Roni, gripping a knife, sneaked into the room.

"Boys, I want you to meet Stan Snyder," said Dixon. "When we needed a look-alike for Charles Parker, photographs were sent to all our field offices. Stan here won the 'contest.' And with a little hair change and makeup, he was our impersonator."

Brian stood with his mouth open. "You mean we haven't found the real Charles Parker?"

"I'm afraid not," answered Springer.

"Oh, but we have," offered Sammy.

Both marshals looked surprised.

"If you found the real Charles Parker," said Springer, "why did you lead Mack Roni here to this house?"

"To help you with your sting operation," said Sammy.

Dixon and Springer looked at each other.

"Detective Ben Phillips was right," said Springer, smiling. "You boys are first rate detectives." A frown wiped out the smile. "What put you on to our plan?"

"It was several things. The boy actor you hired was a little too eager to supply clues and lead us to this house. When I found out the house was rented for only two months, it sounded like a setup. During one of our brainstorming sessions, Brian said, 'Let's pretend.' That helped put the puzzle together. The clues suggested to me that you were pretending to have your relocated witness here."

"If you ever want to become a federal marshal, come and see me," said Dixon.

Sammy pointed to Stan Snyder. "And look at him. He looks too much like Charles Parker to be Charles Parker. The disguised Charles Parker shouldn't look like the real Charles Parker. And I can tell you, the real Charles Parker doesn't look like this man."

Dixon shook his thumb at the steps. "Stan, you can go now. Let me know when everything is clear upstairs."

"You could have rented the house for only one month," said Sammy.

Springer shook his head in agreement. "We didn't know how long this operation was going to last. He shrugged. "Oh, well, it's taxpayers' money."

The look they got from Sammy and Brian made Dixon add, "Maybe the Johnsons will refund part of the money, since we used their house for only two weeks."

"You weren't supposed to discover the house was rented for only a short time," said Springer. "It seems we underestimated Bird-in-Hand's famous detectives. Your reputation is well earned."

Brian stood tall. Now he was ready to shake anybody's hand.

"Maybe I should hire you boys to help me find out how Vincent Bruno learned that Parker was living here at Kitchen Kettle Village," said Dixon. "That's why I'm here. There's a leak. Someone getting the word out, and I haven't been able to find out who."

"So it's happened before?" asked Sammy.

"Once before. Luckily we found out in time."

"How?" asked Sammy.

"Someone tipped off the police."

Sammy looked at Brian and nodded his head. They were remembering the e-mail message they had received.

The action did not go unnoticed by Marshal Dixon. "Why? Do you know something?"

"I imagine you use computers in your line of work," said Sammy.

"Yeah. In fact, I have my laptop with me here on my so-called vacation."

"Do all your men have their own personal computer?" asked Sammy.

"I would think so," answered Dixon.

"So if someone got to one of the computers, they could obtain information about the Witness Protection Program."

"Well, yes, it possible. One of our men could even give someone the information. Look, at this point, I don't want to know *how*. I want to know *who*."

Steve Springer stepped closer to Sammy and in a low voice asked, "Can you really identify our real hidden witness?"

"I believe I can. But if I tell you now, you can deny it."

"Yes, we probably would," answered Dixon honestly.

"So if you two will meet Brian and me at one o'clock tomorrow, I should be able to prove it. Oh, and I might be able to tell you who is leaking your information."

With what they had heard so far, the two marshals couldn't turn down an invitation like that. "Where do you want to meet?" asked Dixon.

"I'll call Pat Burnley when I get home. If she agrees, let's meet at her business office. It's on the second floor of the Jam and Relish Kitchen."

"That's where the frog was kidnapped," said Dixon. "Has it been returned yet?"

Sammy noted Dixon's unusual interest in the frog. "I have a feeling the frog will be back tomorrow morning."

A slight smile signaled Marshal Dixon's delight over Sammy's announcement.

The door opened at the top of the stairs. "Everybody's ready to go, sir."

"You boys have to get home, too," said Dixon. "Can I give you a lift? It's on the way. I'm still staying at the Bird-in-Hand Family Inn."

"We rode our bikes," said Brian.

"No problem. I have a big car," said Dixon.

Brian was still frowning. "What's wrong, Brian?" asked Sammy. "Is there a problem?"

"No, no problem."

Sammy knew better. "Tell me. What is it?"

"You said we were going to reveal the real Charles Parker tomorrow," said Brian.

"Yes, well?"

"I was just wondering. Who's going to kiss the frog?"

CHAPTER THIRTEEN

The gray clouds were either an introduction to a light rain or to a downpour. Regardless of which way the weather went, the farmers would benefit. Sammy didn't mind giving this day to the thirsty crops. After all, green should be the color of summer. So with a smile and raindrops on his face, Sammy pedaled his bike toward the beautiful blooming flowers.

This was the address given to him by Lynne Trout. The colorful array of blossoms was the first clue that he had not miscalculated. The "For-Sale" sign was not for the ranch house in the background but for the bountiful harvest of flower arrangements displayed in front. Ample parking space was provided for the tourists who pulled in off the Old Philadelphia Pike, Rt. 340.

Sammy wasn't sure, but the woman tending the roadside Flower World did look like Lois Parker. The potted plant he bought served two purposes. One was to reward Lynne Trout for her kindness and the other was to put the flower lady in the right frame of mind.

"Do you have a restroom here I can use," asked Sammy, doing a little hopping.

"Usually we don't," said the middle-aged woman, "but since it looks like an emergency, my son over there will take you into the house."

The young boy was about Adam Parker's age. His blond hair and blue eyes added to his friendly smile. He was shy and waited until Sammy spoke first.

"Your mother said you would show me where your restroom is," said Sammy with a touch of urgency in his voice.

The boy headed for the house. "This way."

The boy marched Sammy through the kitchen and the living room to the bathroom off the hallway. The teenage detective didn't see a piano or the picture, but he did see a chair that resembled the one in the picture. The time he spent in the bathroom was enough for Sammy's mood to match that of the gloomy weather outside. He needed more than a chair to prove that Charles Parker lived here.

When he exited the bathroom, a door was slightly ajar to another room off the hall. Sammy's blue eyes sparkled. "I see you have a computer. What kind is it?"

"A Compaq," said the boy, walking from the living room and opening wider the door to the den.

"I have a Macintosh," said Sammy, "but I need a new computer. Is yours hard to operate?"

"It's my dad's. He lets me use it. It's easy. Here, I'll show you."

Soon the computer was on and the monitor was displaying icons. The young boy in the chair was eager to demonstrate his knowledge to the older teen standing by his side.

"How do you get into this program?" asked Sammy pointing to an icon.

The boy clicked the mouse.

The word processor program opened up, revealing—"This program is registered to Charles Parker."

Charles Parker.

The name didn't last long on the screen, one second and it was gone. But it was burned into Sammy's memory. Charles Parker, Charles Parker, Charles Parker.

Sammy was thrilled. He wanted to run out of the house, jump on his bike, and head straight to Kitchen Kettle Village. But the thought of how his findings would affect the boy and his mother made him aware of the consequences of his actions. With some sadness he thanked the boy and said he had to leave.

Because the computer had been his prime focus, he had missed seeing the picture on his way in. It was on the wall to his right, an oil painting of a vase of flowers. And it was signed— Lois Parker.

"My mother painted that," said the boy proudly, never once thinking he was betraying the family's secret.

"It's good, really good," said Sammy, and he left the house.

Sammy picked up his paid-for potted plant, thanked the lady again for the use of the restroom, and hurried to his bike. He slipped a folded raincoat from a side bag and replaced it with the plant. As the rain competed with the raincoat for Sammy's dry clothes, he valued his mother's wisdom of insisting rain gear be standard equipment on a bicycle.

He fought the rain and the traffic as he headed for Kitchen Kettle Village. He looked at his watch. Eleven thirty. His inquiry at the Bird-in-Hand Family Inn earlier had confirmed his suspicions. Because of the call accounting system used to trace phone calls from each room, Manager Rick Meshey was able to give the young detective the information he needed. Now with the newly acquired evidence, Sammy would be ready for the one o'clock appointment.

The Smokehouse Shop sold hickory smoked meats, cured cheese, and cold drinks. The glass-front deli case supplied the makings for delicious cold sandwiches. It also reflected Brian's face, suffering from intense hunger.

"Here comes your friend," said Steve Weaver from behind the counter. Steve was forty-seven, short, with brown hair and a quiet smile. He wore the customary white apron and a red baseball cap. He was surrounded by his three helpers, Betty, Martha, and Judy. After Sammy entered and acknowledged them, they went back to serving the waiting customers.

Sammy and Brian had been in the shop and had interviewed Steve and the women the day before. So it was natural for Brian to suggest they meet in front of the deli counter.

Brian's tortured face, with a struggle, managed to display a grin when he saw Sammy. "Guess what?" he asked. "The frog's back."

"Where is it?" asked Sammy.

"Lynne Trout has it. The frog's back home on the filing cabinet."

"Where did she find the frog?" asked Sammy.

"Hey, can't we eat first, then we can talk," suggested Brian, acting as if he might collapse from starvation.

"Just tell me. Where was the frog found?"

Brian pointed across the street. "The cashier found it this morning. It was on the front counter over at the Jam and Relish Kitchen."

"Oh, really," said Sammy. "Okay, now we can eat."

Sammy and Brian moved closer to the deli counter to await their turn.

CHAPTER FOURTEEN

At one o'clock the boy detectives arrived at the second-floor business office. Inside the conference room, the table was filled with goodies, thanks to Pat Burnley and the office personnel. Sammy handed the potted plant to Lynne. Brian eyed the table of snacks and was about to select a cookie with one hand and pretzels with the other when Pat called him away. She introduced the boys to her son, Mike, who was the president of Kitchen Kettle Village, and to her daughter, Joanne, who was vice president.

The night before, Pat had agreed with Sammy that a meeting was in order. She needed to discuss her new advertising ideas. And should the frog be returned in the morning, why not celebrate?

Many shop owners and service employees had been invited to the "social." Yummy, the Gingerbread Man, was there along with John, the candle man. Marshal Dixon was munching on a cookie. Steve Weaver, from the Smokehouse, minus his white apron, drifted in from Lynne's office. Al and Linda Lowrey from the Grande-Place were wondering why the return of the frog warranted this much attention.

Lynne, with the biggest smile, suddenly entered the room and announced, "Here she is, back where she belongs." The receptionist, having a tight grip on her green friend, raised the frog into the air.

"Welcome home," said Pat. "Now we can get started on our new catalog campaign."

Sammy gave the frog a quick inspection. He smiled and said, "May I hold the frog?"

Lynne lowered the green figure and carefully placed it into Sammy's waiting hands. The teenage detective noticed the frog had a solid base. He glanced over at Harry Clover who just stepped into the crowded room. "Harry, can you get me a drill with a one-eighth inch drill bit and a hammer?"

"I think I can find them somewhere. Be right back."

Marshall Steve Springer, who just arrived, stepped aside at the door to allow Harry to pass. "Sorry, if I'm late," he said to no one special.

Brian took his eyes from the dish of cookies long enough to inspect the frog. "It's bigger than I thought it would be." Then he whispered into Sammy's ear, "What are you going to do with the hammer and drill?"

"I want to satisfy my curiosity," said Sammy.

"You need a hammer and drill to satisfy your curiosity?" said Brian. His head turned and nodded at the table. "All I need is a cookie."

Ignoring his friend's comment, Sammy said, "While we're waiting for Harry to return, Marshal Dixon, why don't you explain to the people why we're here."

"Be glad to," said Dixon. "Some time within the last year, federal marshals representing the courts placed a family here in your area. The man gave testimony in court that convicted a banker who was laundering money. The banker took money made in gambling and drugs and invested it in legitimate businesses. In other words, the banker took dirty money and made it appear clean."

Brian, wanting to feel part of the team, said, "That banker was Vincent Bruno. Right, Marshal Dixon?"

Dixon nodded. "Vincent Bruno, who was sentenced to jail, threatened the life of the witness. It then became our job to give the witness and his family protection. We changed their appearance, gave them new identities, and relocated them here."

"In my opinion," said Sammy, "the witness was brave to testify, knowing that he and his family would have to move to a different state and assume new identities."

"And," added Brian, "living with the idea that someone is out there to get him."

Dixon pulled on his suit coat to take out any wrinkles and gave a little cough. "Last night, with the help of Sammy Wilson and Brian Helm, we took that threat away. We captured the man sent here to harm the witness."

"He was Mack Roni," said Brian, "the man who broke into your shop, Mr. Lowrey."

Marshal Dixon slid some fingers over his bushy eyebrows and coughed again. "Now, previously, Marshal Springer had challenged your local amateur detectives to find our hidden witness. The real reason we are all here today is for them to identify our witness if they can." He tugged at the back of his coat, gave a give-us-what-you-got look at Sammy, and said no more.

"What about the frog?" asked John, the candle man.

"I may be able to explain both cases," announced Sammy.

"Here they are," interrupted Harry as he dashed in out of breath. He clutched both a drill and a hammer.

Sammy went over to Marshal Springer and handed him the frog. "Before I reveal the real Charles Parker, let's have a look at the frog. Will you hold this while I plug in the drill?"

"You're not going to hurt the frog are you?" asked Lynne, whose large eyes were on the drill.

Sammy inserted the plug into the wall. "Mrs. Burnley, you told me before that the Village originally had two identical frogs."

"Yes, we had two, one for the pond and one for my granddaughter," said Pat.

"You also said you filled one frog with candy. And yet the frog Marshal Springer is holding is solid."

"Yes," said Lynne. "I wondered about that when I rescued the frog from the pond."

Sammy rubbed a finger nail across the solid bottom. White powder collected under his nail. "I'm curious as to why this plaster filling has been added to the frog. What I want to do, Lynne, is drill small holes all around the edge of the filled area. Then we should be able to break the extra plaster loose from inside the frog itself. Is that okay with you?"

"Yeah, I guess. You have me curious now," said Lynne.

"Marshal, if you'll hold the frog sideways, I'll drill the holes," said Sammy.

By drilling the holes close together and wiggling the drill, the thin wall between each hole gave way. The porous plaster crumbled easily. The result was a circle cut around the filled-in area. A light tap with the hammer caused the big lump of plaster to fall into Sammy's hand.

No one in the room made a sound. Everyone's attention was on the clump of dry plaster. Was it just plaster? Was it added to give more weight to the frog? Or did it contain a mysterious object?

Sammy knelt and placed the chunk of plaster on the floor. He lifted the hammer over the plaster. Brian was hoping his friend was not about to make a fool of himself. Sammy was thinking the same thing as he smashed the hammer into the plaster. The large lump shattered into various-sized pieces. In the center of the crumbled mess lay a shiny object.

"Don't touch that," shouted Dixon.

Eyes were on Dixon as he knelt beside Sammy. Very slowly and carefully he pinched the metallic object by its edge and lifted it for close examination. "I'd say this is a safety deposit box key. I've been looking for something like this since since we took Charles Parker into our Witness Protection Program."

"You mean Mr. Parker really did steal money from the bank?" asked Brian

"Looks that way. The F.B.I. will check the key for prints. They'll also be able to trace the key back to its bank and recover the stolen money." Dixon looked at Springer. "Don't let anyone out of the room."

Steve Springer handed the now hollow frog to Lynne and stood at the open doorway.

"Well, Sammy and Brian, are you prepared to identify Charles Parker before we take him with us?" asked Marshal Dixon.

"We are," said Sammy. "According to my partner here, somebody put a spell on Charles Parker and changed him into a frog. Now, if he's right, all we have to do is break the spell. Lynne, what do you think will break the spell?"

Lynne frowned. "You want me to kiss the frog, don't you?"

"It would help," said Sammy, smiling.

Brian shifted his position and stood behind a particular person.

Very slowly, the receptionist raised the frog to her face. She took a good look at the frog. It would be the widest mouth she ever kissed.

Some of the people giggled. Others made a face. And the rest just gazed, half expecting the prince, in the form of Charles Parker, to appear.

"I believe. I believe," said Lynne theatrically, and she kissed the frog.

At the same time, unseen by anyone, Brian pinched the rear of the man in front of him.

The man jumped into the air, raising his arms. "Wow!" he yelled.

Everybody in the room stared at the man but couldn't believe it. The maintenance man had always been a quiet person.

"Harry Clover? He's the hidden witness?" asked Lynne.

"Yes, he's Charles Parker," said Sammy.

"Well, I have only one thing to say," said Lynne. "My husband never reacts like that when I kiss him."

Most everyone laughed. Charles Parker, alias Harry Clover, did not. Charles was rubbing his rear end. This day had come crashing down around him. He had lost everything. He would never see the money he had taken from the bank—

the money he had stashed away in a safety deposit box.

Pat Burnley looked at the maintenance man she knew as Harry Clover. "Is it true?" she wanted to know. "Are you this Charles Parker fellow?"

Charles glanced at Marshal Springer looking for an okay. He got it. "Yes, it's true. I'm Charles Parker."

"How did you figure it out, Sammy?" asked Dixon.

"At first it was the relationship Marshal Springer seemed to have with Harry Clover. Sorry, I mean with Charles Parker. Springer knew Charles Parker had an appointment with us about the kidnapped frog." Sammy looked at Springer. "Remember? You said that Harry wanted to fool someone. You must have had some kind of contact with him in order to know that. Because according to Harry or Charles, his hiring us as a joke, was to be a secret."

Marshal Springer lowered his head.

Sammy continued. "Then when we arrived over an hour late for the appointment with Charles, he apologized for being late. He knew we were to be detained for an hour or two. I would guess that Springer informed Charles of the sting operation and our involvement in it."

"I'm impressed," said Dixon.

"Another small test I conducted was having Charles respond to the name, Chuck. My friend, Brian, reminded me that Chuck is a nickname for Charles. The other day when Charles was within hearing distance, I said that Yummy should *chuck* his hot costume. Charles automatically reacted to the nickname as he had been conditioned to do all his life."

"That's something we can't change when we remake a relocated witness," said Dixon.

"The concrete proof came when Brian and I obtained an illustrated newspaper article about Charles' wife having a flower business at home. We got the news item over the Internet. And in the photograph we saw a chair and a picture on a wall. I saw that same chair and that same picture in Charles Parker's house this morning."

"You were in my house?" asked Parker with a surprised look.

"At your wife's invitation," replied Sammy.

"But that chair and painting could be in anyone's home," said Dixon.

"The chair, yes. But not an original oil painting signed Lois Parker."

Dixon pulled out a pocket computer, snapped it open, and made an electronic note to himself.

"Here's another suggestion you can add to your computerized list, marshal," said Sammy. "When a relocated witness with a new identity takes his computer with him, be sure his old name is deleted from the registered ownership of each program on the hard disc."

Dixon smiled, shook his head, and pecked away at the small buttons.

"Now, what about the frog?" asked Springer.

"I suspected more than playing a joke was involved," said Sammy. "If Charles wanted to tease the person who took the frog, simpler ways were available. Also, when Charles talked to us after we started to investigate the case, he always asked if we had found the frog. Not, 'Do you know who took the frog?' He was more interested in the frog than in the person who took it. So I suspected he hired us because he really wanted the frog returned. But I wondered why? What was so special about the frog?"

Lynne turned the frog over. "How did you know a key was inside here?"

"I didn't. It wasn't until you brought the frog into this room and held it up that I knew someone had tampered with it." Sammy looked at Charles. "Why did you put the key into the frog in the first place?"

Charles Parker took a deep breath. He knew if he answered Sammy's question he was admitting his guilt. He appeared relieved that the deception was over. "I was the only person who knew the truth about the money," he said. "I had the key in my pocket. I couldn't keep it at home because my wife or son might find it. I knew if it got into the marshal's hands, I would be out of the protection program and in jail. One day when I was working on the stone wall near the pond, I saw the frog. I decided the key would be safer there than in my pocket. So I took the frog, mixed some patching plaster, and buried the key inside. When the plaster dried I replaced the frog into the pond."

Brian stood closer to the snack table.

"Charles," said Pat Burnley, "when Lynne rescued the frog from the dismantled pond, why didn't you do something about the frog then?"

"Lynne got to the frog before I could. She said she was going to keep it in the office." Charles shrugged. "So I thought, Hey, why not? The key would be safe there until I needed it. But when the frog was taken, I got worried. I didn't know where it would end up. So I decided that when the frog was returned, I'd bury the key under an engraved brick in the walkway. It would be safer there."

"So what's going to happen to Charles now?" asked Sammy, looking at Dixon.

Marshal Dixon shrugged. "That will be up to the courts. I have no say in Charles' future."

Sammy was thinking of Charles' wife and son when he asked, "Couldn't you and Springer put a good word in for him? You have the deposit box key. You'll get the dirty money back."

Dixon shook his head. "I'm sorry, but Charles stole the money. He lied to us. He broke the law. He must pay for his actions. There will be no favoritism shown here."

"What if it was your son?" asked Sammy.

Dixon's face became tense. "What do you mean?"

"Your son was arrested last year for threatening a bookie," said Sammy. "I think you had some words with the bookie and the assault charges were dropped."

Dixon's face was now red. "Sammy, if you know that, then you know my son used a wooden gun. There was really no harm done."

"I don't see any harm done here either. No one was hurt."

"That's right," said some of those present. In the short time they had known Charles Parker as Harry Clover, he had been a decent person.

Brian added his two cents. "All Charles did was liberate some mob money before it was sent to other banks." Brian raised and spread his arms as though he was delivering a plea in a courtroom. Crumbs fell from his fingers. "Did Harry spend that money on himself or on his family? No, he did not. His only crime was to take that money away from criminals. He kept that tainted money from being used. He put it into a safety deposit box for safe keeping, until he could . . . he could . . . hand the key over to you."

Sammy grabbed and squeezed one of Brian's arms and lowered it, hoping the other arm would follow. Sammy didn't need Brian's theatrics. He had another way to convince Dixon. "Marshal, you wanted to know who leaked the information about Charles Parker being at Kitchen Kettle Village."

Both marshals nodded their heads.

"Well, let me tell you a story. Once upon a time a curse was put on a nineteen-year-old boy. The cause of the curse was lack of love and loneliness. But unlike the story where a curse changed a prince into a frog, the boy was changed into a gambler. All the boy could think about was gambling—playing the horses and betting on sport games. One day the boy found himself so much in debt to the bookies, he wanted to commit suicide. One of the bookies came to the boy and said, 'Your father is a federal marshal. If you can get us some valuable information from him, we will cancel your debt.' Later that night while the boy was thinking about what the bookie had said, he saw his father's laptop computer lying on the sofa." Sammy paused and with a sympathetic look asked, "Do I have to continue the story?"

Dixon shook his head. "No, I get the message." He paused and reflected on all that had happened in the last couple of days. He headed for the door. "Come on, Springer. Let's go."

Marshal Springer grabbed hold of Charles Parker.

Dixon held up his hands, "No, no, let him stay." Dixon looked at Charles. "Just don't leave town."

Brian elbowed his friend and whispered, "Was it Dixon's son, Glen Junior, who sent us the e-mail?"

"Yes. When I studied the message, it contained gambler expressions like 'taking a chance,' 'you can bet on that,' and 'before his luck runs out.' And using the name fedwell, I figured Junior used his father's computer to send the e-mail. I checked at the Family Inn and a call had gone out from their room to the Internet service provider at the time indicated on my e-mail message."

"I guess Glen Junior felt guilty supplying Charles Parker's location to pay off his gambling debt," said Brian.

"Yeah," said Sammy. "Guilt has a way of gnawing at you."

As the marshals' footsteps faded down the stairway, Charles Parker felt alone, nervous. It was an awkward moment. The room was quiet. Everyone was staring at him. He glanced at the floor. He could feel the pressure of all the eyes. What were they thinking? What kind of future would he have?

Pat Burnley looked at the man she knew as Harry Clover, model employee. His skilled hands had constructed and repaired many projects in the ten months he had been at the Village. Pat didn't need to think about it long. She smiled. "Harry Clover, don't you have work to do?"

Charles Parker looked up and saw forgiving faces. He came into this room as Harry Clover, they were allowing him to leave the same way. "Yes, I have bricks to lay," he said and hurried down the steps before they changed their minds. Difficult days lay ahead. He would be held accountable for taking the money. But right now he did have work to do.

Brian's mouth was attacking a chocolate chip cookie when John, the candle man, yelled, "Who kidnapped the frog?"

"Yeah, who took the frog?" asked the others.

"It's still a mystery," said Lynne Trout. "But here's a note left with the frog when she was returned this morning."

"What does it say?" asked Brian between bites.

Lynne read from the paper. "I'm returning the frog early, but you owe me the ransom. A bag of lollipops."

Everyone laughed.

Steve Weaver from The Smokehouse Shop said, "John, that sounds like something you'd do."

"Me? How about you? I heard your special for today was to be extra crispy, smoked frog legs."

"Well, anyway I'm happy the frog was returned," said Lynne, "but I'm sad you detectives weren't able to solve the case." Her tone was a playful tease.

"Oh, but we do know who kidnapped the frog," said Sammy, surprising everyone.

Brian coughed out some crumbs. "We do?"

"Where was the frog found this morning?" asked Sammy.

"Pam found it on the front counter downstairs," answered Pat.

Sammy consulted his notebook to make sure. After skimming several pages, he looked at Lynne. "Lynne, you kidnapped the frog."

Even though it was done in fun as a joke, Lynne was genuinely surprised at Sammy's announcement. "You boys really are good," she said.

"You snatched the frog, Lynne?" teased John.

"Yes, I did."

"Why?" asked, Steve Weaver.

"Complacency," answered Lynne. "We get too set in our ways, too pleased with ourselves. I wanted to shake things up around here."

"Well, it worked," said Brian. "You shook the frog and the key fell out. That shook up Charles Parker and he confessed to taking the money. Sammy's fairy tale shook up Marshal Dixon. And—"

"Brian, we get the idea," interrupted Sammy. "Come on. We have to go now."

"Oh, no, you don't," said Pat. "Before you go, you must tell us how you knew Lynne took the frog."

"Yesterday, I told everyone that you wanted the frog returned to be photographed for your catalog. I said they could secretly return the frog when nobody was watching. Then I told them where to leave the frog."

"So, if they dropped off the frog without anyone seeing them," said John, "how do you know Lynne took it?"

Sammy grinned. "I gave everyone a different place to return the frog. I listed the different places with the people's names in my notebook."

"Yeah, that's clever," said John. "You told me if I took it, I was to put the frog on the bench in front of this building. Here I thought you were telling everyone to put the frog on the same bench."

"He told me on the steps," yelled someone.

Sammy raised his hand. "It was nice meeting all of you people. I hope Brian and I are leaving Kitchen Kettle Village as it was when we first entered it." Sammy pulled Brian by the arm towards the doorway. The popcorn in Brian's other hand went with them.

"Thank you," said Pat. "Please come back and see us."

"Hey, did you hear that, Sammy," said Brian as he tried twisting his arm from his friend's grip. "I'm going back for some cookies."

"No, you're not," said Sammy, pulling Brian half way down the steps.

"But, I wanted a cookie," he said. Then he eyed the crackers and the sample jelly on the displays below. "Never mind," said Brian.

SAMMY AND BRIAN MYSTERY SERIES

#1 **The Quilted Message** by Ken Munro

The whole village was talking about it. Did the Amish quilt contain more than just twenty mysterious cloth pictures? The pressure was on for Bird-in-Hand's two teenage detectives, Sammy and Brian, to solve the mystery. Was Amos King murdered because of the quilt? Who broke into the country store? It was time for Sammy and Brian to unmask the intruder. $4.95

#2 **Bird in the Hand** by Ken Munro

When arson is suspected on an Amish farm, the village of Bird-in-Hand responds with a fund-raiser. The appearance of a mysterious tattooed man starts a series of events that ends in murder. And who is The Bird? Sammy and Brian are bound hand and foot by the feathered creature. Bird-in-Hand's own teenage sleuths break free and unravel the mystery. $5.95

#3 **Amish Justice** by Ken Munro

The duo turns into a trio when Joyce Myers becomes the newest member of the Sammy and Brian detective team. Is farmland in Lancaster County worth killing for? Frank Crawford thinks so. And when the police call the attempts on his life accidents, the old farmer sends for the teenage detectives. The three sleuths soon discover one of five suspects knows about the "IT" under the house. $5.95

#4 **Jonathan's Journal** by Ken Munro

After Scott Boyer comes to town, a young girl disappears. He then makes an offer Sammy and Brian can't refuse. A 200-year-old journal holds a challenge of a lifetime. It holds two secrets: a mysterious puzzle and murder. Bird-in-Hand's super detectives investigate the meaning behind its cryptic message. $5.95

#5 **Doom Buggy** by Ken Munro

An Amish buggy disappears. Twenty cut-out letters appear in its place. Then someone wants George Brock dead—in his welding shop. Sammy, Brian, and Joyce, fifteen-year-old sleuths from Bird-in-Hand, try to find the connection between these three mysterious happenings. $5.95

#6 **Fright Train** by Ken Munro

The actor, John Davenport, retires in Strasburg. He brings with him Manaus, the monster from his cult movie, *Fright Train*. While riding the Strasburg Railroad, Sammy and Brian learn that someone wants to steal something from the actor. But what? Is it his autobiography manuscript? Or is it the "Fright Train"? $5.95

— —

These books may be purchased at your local bookstore or ordered from Gaslight Publishers, P. O. Box 258, Bird-in-Hand, PA 17505.

Enclosed is $_____(please add $2.00 for shipping and handling). Send check or money order only.

Name_____

Address _____

City_____ State_____ Zip Code_____